STARVATION CAMP

When Corporal Zachary McQuestion veered off his icy route in the Yukon, he was eagerly anticipating the warmth and comfort he'd always found at Molly Malone's. What he finds in her cabin, however, makes his blood boil: intruders have murdered Molly for her meager provisions—little more than a few bags of flour.

Now, the corporal vows to find Molly's murderers and bring them to justice—even if it means tracking them through frozen wilderness and reliving his own tortured past . . .

STARVATION CAMP

Bill Pronzini

GUNSMOKE

First published in the UK by Hale

This hardback edition 2008
by BBC Audiobooks Ltd
by arrangement with
Golden West Literary Agency

ISBN 978 1 405 68198 8

British Library Cataloguing in Publication Data available.

Printed and bound in Great Britain by
Antony Rowe Ltd., Chippenham, Wiltshire

*For Bernie Nalaboff—Western fan numero uno,
who also likes a "Northern" now and then*

STARVATION CAMP

CHAPTER 1

THERE WAS SOMETHING wrong at Molly Malone's roadhouse.

McQuestion sensed it as soon as he came in sight of the two-story log building set back off the Dawson trail, where the Chandindu and Yukon rivers intersected. In the dark Arctic sky behind it, the northern lights—rose, pearl, blue—pulsed and trembled in what the Siwash called "the dance of the spirits"—the souls of the dead at play. But no lamplight showed behind the roadhouse's hoarfrosted window, and it would have if everything was as it should be inside.

Quickly he mushed his dogs off the river ice and across to within a few yards of the front door. He saw nothing, heard nothing except for the faint keening of the wind. Still, he slid a mittened hand inside his parka, unsnapped the holster flap covering his revolver. Then he gave the dogs a command to lie down, waited until they obeyed, and stepped off the sledge's runners.

As far as he could see, the snow around the cabin was unmarked. But there had been a flurry a couple of hours earlier, only just quit, and it would have covered any tracks made up to that time. He slogged to the door, took off both mittens and his snowshoes when he reached it. The door wasn't barred; when he tugged at the drawstring latch, the wind pushed the heavy timber inward a few inches.

McQuestion drew his revolver and moved inside, using his shoulder to ease the door shut behind him. Across the deep-shadowed common room he could make out the shape of the potbellied stove. Molly's two Siwash helpers always kept that stove stoked with coal during the winter months, so that it glowed bright red and kept the room summer-warm. But the room was cold now. The stove hadn't been tended in several hours.

"Molly!" he called. "Hello, Molly!"

No answer.

"Molly, it's Zack!"

Silence, heavy and unbroken.

The feeling of wrongness crawled on McQuestion's neck like a stinging brule fly. He moved sideways to the window, sliding his fingers along the rough surface of the wall until they found the shelf where Molly kept her night lantern, the one that until tonight had always burned a welcome to sourdoughs and other travelers. The lantern was there, cold to the touch. So was a block of wooden matches. McQuestion snapped off one of the sticks, scraped it alight one-handed, and lit the wick.

The lamp glow crowded darkness into the corners of the big room. At the first sweep of McQuestion's gaze, everything seemed normal enough. The tables and chairs grouped near the stove and in the dining room beyond were all in place; the plank bar was empty and polished to a shine; there was nothing on the whipsawed floor that didn't belong there. But the second time he scanned the interior, carrying the lantern and moving away from the window, he began to notice the things that were wrong. The shelf behind the bar where Molly kept her whiskey and seegars was empty. In the dining room, the bowl of applesauce made from dried apples and given free to anyone who bought a meal from her, as a benevolence against scurvy, had been spilled on one of the tables. The daguerreotype of Molly's folks and the chalkboard that said "MUTTON AND THE FIXIN'S— $3.50" had been knocked askew on the rear wall, as if someone had been thrown up hard against the logs.

McQuestion's eyes took on a dark, feral shine; tension made a vein bulge in one temple. He entered the dining room. From there the lantern let him see into the side alcove where the coal cookstove and larder were. A sack of flour had burst on the larder floor, leaving a fan of white across it like a fine sifting of snow; footprints tracked through it to and from the outside rear door that opened off the larder. When he moved closer he saw that the shelves had been stripped of Molly's food supply. Not a single sack or box or tin remained.

Immediately he veered to the left, beyond the cookstove, to the closed door of Molly's bedroom. He yanked it open. The room was empty, everything within as neatly arranged as he remembered it, Molly's guitar in its customary place at the foot of her bed. Without entering, he reversed direction and moved back through the dining room and across the common room, hurrying now, and climbed the narrow staircase butted against the front wall. The whole of the second floor ran to bunk space—two long rows on either side of a center walkway, with each bunk curtained off for privacy. He went the full length of the room, holding the lantern high, looking left, right, left, right. None of the bunks was occupied, and except for two at the rear, where the Siwash helpers slept, there was no sign that any of them had been used recently.

There was nowhere else to look inside the road-house proper. In the clearing in back were three out-buildings: an animal shelter, a storage shed, and the privy. He hurried downstairs, set the lantern under the window, and went out with his revolver still drawn.

It was snowing again, just a light swirl of flakes; the wind felt icy against his bare hand. But it was mid-March, and with the temperature up around zero, there was no immediate risk of frostbite or of skin freezing to metal. The dogs were still lying quietly, all except Takus, with heads tucked down; the Siberian stirred in the lead traces, watching Mc-Question as he tramped away from the door. McQuestion paid no attention. Takus was hungry but he was also well trained; he wouldn't move until he was told to, and he wouldn't let the male-mutes move either.

The nearest outbuilding was the privy, set opposite the rear door to the roadhouse. McQuestion bypassed it without stopping and slogged toward the low, squat shape of the shed. The flickering pulse of the north-lights, made even more eerie by the whorls of falling snow, lit up the sky above it. Somewhere in the spruce woods beyond, a wolf set up a mournful bay-ing as if in protest against the constant fireworks dis-play. The dogs instantly began an answering chorus.

When he was within ten yards of the shed door he stopped. And he knew, staring ahead at it, what he would find inside the shed. It had nothing to do with any of his senses; it was a sudden intuitive knowledge, hard and sharp like a dagger of ice stabbing into his mind. He stood still for close to a minute, steeling himself, with the snow whipping around him. Then he holstered his revolver, slowly crossed the remaining distance to the shed, and shoved open the door.

In the darkness within, all he could make out was a series of indistinct shapes. He entered, wedged the door shut, found a match in one of his pockets, and thumbed it alight. The yellow flare let him see the whole of the shed's interior—the frozen moose meat that was sold as dog food for a dollar a pound, the axes and other tools, and the corpses of Molly Malone and the two Siwash thrown against one another on the icy floor.

The match guttered, went out. McQuestion said, "Christ!" in a thick, choked voice and struck another match, cupping it in both hands to steady it. Then he hunkered down with the light. There was a frozen crimson stain, shaped like a small beefsteak, on the front of Molly's sweater; the cloth around the wound was scorched with black powder. Without looking at her face or the stiffened strands of blond hair that covered it, he shifted the matchlight to the bodies of the two Indians. Before it flickered out he was able to tell that they, too, had been shot at close range.

He straightened, his lips pulled in flat against his teeth, the taste of gunmetal in his mouth. He left the shed, retraced his path to the front door of the roadhouse. Inside, he carried the lighted lantern into the larder and examined the footprints in the flour spill. As near as he could tell, there were two sets of them. He took this to mean that the flour sack had been dropped after Molly and her helpers were killed. And that it had been two men who'd done it. But that was all the tracks told him; there was nothing distinctive about either set.

As he started out of the larder, he noticed a small piece of cloth caught on a protruding shelf nail two feet above the floor. He plucked it free. Nankeen cloth, brown, probably from a pair of trousers— cheap material and unsuited to the Far North. The kind of clothing a cheechako would buy in Seattle or one of the other outfitting centers Outside. Mc-Question put the fragment into the breast pocket of his uniform tunic and then set about searching the rest of the premises.

He found nothing in the alcove, the dining room, or Molly's bedroom. In the common room, on the floor behind the plank bar, was a seegar that had been lost from one of the boxes and accidentally crushed underfoot. When he bent to look at the seegar, something wedged against one of the hogsheads supporting the plank glittered in the lantern light. He reached out and picked it up.

It was a shiny gold watch fob, shaped like an anvil, with a horseshoe on one side that had the words "GOOD LUCK" imprinted on it; on the other side, cut into a tiny metal plate, was the name "FLOYD." There was no dust on the fob, as there would have been if it had lain on the floor for any length of time. McQuestion tuned it over in his fingers, studying it. Then he tucked it away in the same uniform pocket with the piece of nankeen.

The common room yielded nothing else; neither did any of the bunks on the upper floor. The cloth, the fob, and the apparent fact that he would be looking for two men with at least one and maybe two heavily loaded sleds were little enough to go on, but he had started with less before.

There was nothing more to be done here, not by him; it was time to leave. Spending the night in the roadhouse, after what had happened, was out of the question. He hunted up a grease pencil, a two-foot-square piece of heavy butcher paper, and a roll of black tape and carried these to one of the dining-room tables. On the paper in large block letters he wrote:

THIS ESTABLISHMENT CLOSED UNTIL FURTHER NOTICE. NO ADMITTANCE UNDER PENALTY OF THE LAW.

CORPORAL ZACHARY MCQUESTION
NORTH WEST MOUNTED POLICE

He took the paper and tape into the common room and put the sign up in the window. Even with the hoarfrost that clung to the outer side of the glass, it could be read by anyone venturing up close enough. He slid the locking bar into its brackets on either side of the door, made sure it was secure, then left the building through the rear door. Securing that door was more of a problem; he settled for wedging a length of cut wood against the latch and packing snow around it. That would keep the wind from pulling it open and letting animals inside, at least.

The dogs were tired and hungry and they began snapping at one another when he roused them. Takus, the leader, controlled them and got them moving. But McQuestion didn't take the team far, just two hundred yards or so upstream along the Yukon and into a copse of spruce. He could still see the roadhouse from there, a dark looming silhouette against the waning streaks and arches of the north-lights.

He unpacked his trail ax and cut and trimmed wood for a fire. He swung the ax in short, hard, savage strokes, working off some of his pent-up rage, exhausting himself so he would be able to sleep later on. He did not think of Molly as he worked, but she was there in his mind just the same.

When he had enough wood he tied the caribou

sled sheet between two trees five feet apart, at an angle into the wind, and anchored the bottom with one of the logs he'd cut. He built his fire another five feet in front of the blanket, fed it until it was blazing. Then he piled spruce boughs between the fire and the sled sheet, making himself a bed for the night.

After unharnessing the dogs, he filled their kettle with snow and started a separate fire for it and to unthaw the last of the stringy moose meat he carried for them. He changed his footwear, putting on caribou socks with the hair inside to protect his feet, then packed out his grub even though he had no appetite. What he wanted just then was a drink of whiskey—several drinks. But even if he had had a bottle with him, he would not have opened it; no one but a cheechako ever touched liquor on the trail in winter, because it made it impossible for one to withstand the cold. Liquor didn't mix with sorrow and hate, either. And as far as food went, you ate in the wilderness whether you were hungry or not. Eating wasn't a matter of appetite; it was a matter of survival.

He put the last of his bacon on to fry, and his snow-filled billycan on to boil for tea. Inside his nearly empty flour sack he formed a hollow in what was left of the flour, put in salt and baking powder and melted snow from the billy, and stirred up a ball of dough. This he fried in the hot bacon fat, along with a handful of frozen beans.

The food seemed to clog in his throat when he ate; he had to keep washing it down with swallows of tea. The dogs had set up a howling by the time he was finished. He fed and watered them, got them bedded down in the snow near the fire with their backs to the wind. Then he fueled the fire again and lay down on the spruce boughs with his old buffalo robe over him. With the wind blowing heat into the shelter of the sled sheet, he was warm enough. Or he would have been on any other night. The cold was in the marrow of his bones tonight.

Sleep was a long time coming. The firelight created restless shadows in the nearby trees; the smoke rose straight up until it cooled, then spread out to form a canopy. From the river he could hear the low boom of shifting ice, a heavy counterpoint to the hiss and crackle of the fire. Molly was sharp in his thoughts now; he could no longer shut her out. But Eileen was there, too, as she often was. And the faceless men who had killed Molly were joined by that other faceless man, the one who had been responsible for Eileen's death—the man he knew only as George Blanton.

When he finally slept he was plagued by dreams, ugly dreams, and once he sat bolt upright with the river voice still pounding in his ears. He stared out again at the dark distant shape of the roadhouse.

"I'll find them, Molly," he said aloud—words similar to others he had spoken five years ago. "I'll find them!"

CHAPTER 2

MCQUESTION REACHED DAWSON City midmorning of the next day, with the body of Molly Malone wrapped in a blanket and roped to his sledge. He had left the corpses of the two Siwash where they lay inside the storage shed; they would be safe enough there from foraging animals until someone from B Division headquarters saw to their burial.

Dawson was situated at the confluence of the Yukon and Klondike rivers, the best natural town site in the Territory. It was shaped like a flatiron, the nose of which pointed upstream and ended in high bluffs; most of the buildings faced the Yukon, with a range of hills on the other side, dominated by Midnight Dome, that extended back to where the Klondike cut across at the heel and flowed into the Yukon. Up until a year and a half before, when a white man named George Carmack and two Indians, Tagish Charlie and Skookum Jim, first discovered gold on Rabbit (now Bonanza) Creek, there hadn't been a town here at all. It was only after news of the strike reached Forty-Mile and the miners abandoned the settlement they called "the other end of nowhere" and rushed upstream that a trader named Joe Ladue built a sawmill and a cabin on the site and established the town in honor of an explorer named George M. Dawson. Sixteen months ago, in November of '96, when McQuestion had been transferred here from Alberta, everyone in Dawson was living in tents and the only other finished building was a saloon. Now there were some three dozen commercial structures lining Front Street, the main thoroughfare—and this in spite of the fact that much of the town had been destroyed by fire late last autumn. More buildings were going up on side streets and along the riverfront, many of them private dwellings. Even the number of shanties in Lousetown, across the Klondike, had increased.

And the town would swell again, to two or three times its present size, when the river-ice breakup came in early May and more stampeders poured in. Thousands of new gold seekers were massed at Lake Bennett and Lake Lindeman, waiting for the warm chinook winds to blow and the ice to begin to move on the Yukon. Still more continued to stream over Chilkoot and White passes from Alaska—a gold-hungry human chain floundering through treacherous ice and snow.

Come summer, Dawson would become a full-fledged, hell-raising boomtown. As soon as the paddle-wheelers were able to make the trip downstream from Whitehorse, their passengers would include scores of cardsharps, sure-thing men, thugs, and whores. The Alaskan town of Skagway, one of the two Panhandle ports where steamers from Seattle and other points Outside deposited the stampeders, was already in the hands of a confidence man named Soapy Smith and his band of cutthroats; countless cheechakos had already been robbed, beaten, and murdered in the past several months, and because of Skagway's isolation there seemed to be no immediate end to it. The Mounted Police were determined to keep a similar brand of lawlessness from spawning on Canadian soil, even though law enforcement in the Yukon was anything but easy. There were only a few hundred Redcoats in the Territory, most of whom were strung out along four hundred miles of the Yukon River and the Alaska frontier.

Still, with all the problems posed by the rush, every Redcoat McQuestion knew looked forward to breakup. The reason was the shortage of food. In Dawson store shelves and the warehouses of the trading companies were near empty; the fire on

Thanksgiving Day had destroyed what should have been a surplus of supplies in the town. Prices had risen to dangerous highs—a dollar and a half a pound for bacon, a dollar a pound for beans, a hundred dollars for a sack of flour. One sourdough at Stewart River had died of starvation. Dozens of others were suffering from scurvy. Dog owners at the more isolated of the outlying creeks had taken to killing and eating their animals; others were feeding theirs boiled green hides and would likely follow suit in the slaughter before the ice began to move. There had been one fatal shooting as the result of an argument over a can of stewed tomatoes, plus any number of lesser skirmishes. Conditions were approaching those of a starvation camp. And the fear was that if breakup came late this year, hungry miners would storm the depleted trading company warehouses and the stores at Fort Cudahy, Forty-Mile, and other outposts; that there would be food riots in which dozens would be injured or killed.

It was the food shortage that was on McQuestion's mind as he mushed his dogs past the remains of an icebound scow and up onto shore. It had been on his mind all morning. Molly and her two helpers had been murdered for her supply of food and whiskey; he could see no other possible reason for the shootings. Molly had been too easygoing, too generous, to make enemies during the two years she'd been in the Yukon, and she had kept nothing of value at the roadhouse. The dust and nuggets she collected from her customers were sent to the Alaska Commercial Company in Dawson once a week for safekeeping. This was common knowledge.

Murdered for tins of mutton and beef, slabs of fat bacon, sacks of flour and beans and potatoes. Three people murdered for *food*—by men whose bellies Molly would have filled on credit if they couldn't pay, because that was the kind of soft-hearted woman she'd been . . .

McQuestion drove his team along the frozen mud on Front Street, toward the Mounted Police barracks at its foot. There had been no snowfall this morning, the temperature was still around zero, and the edge of the sun was about to peer up over the horizon for its daily few hours of visibility—all they had seen of it for months and all they would see of it for a while yet to come. The shadowed street was crowded with miners on their way to and from the surrounding goldfields. In front of the Tivoli Saloon and Gambling House, two dead malemutes lay side by side with their heads half blown away. Both were frozen solid. With the food situation as bad as it was, McQuestion was surprised someone hadn't made off with the carcasses as soon as they were shot.

When he reached the barracks he took his sledge

around to the kennels at the rear. Another Redcoat was feeding a dozen of the howling and barking Queen's dogs; he told McQuestion that Colonel Steele, the commander of B Division and of all the Mounted Police in Yukon Territory, was in his office. McQuestion used two terse sentences to explain what he carried under the robe on his sledge. Then he entered the barracks, knocked on the door to the OC's office.

Colonel Samuel B. Steele was something of a legend in the Force. He had helped to organize it, to shape its policies. One of his half-dozen heroic acts had been to lead the federal militia in crushing the bloody Saskatchewan rebellion of Louis Riel and his Metís separatists in '85. Now, he was here in the Yukon to keep peace during the stampede. He had succeeded thus far—Dawson and the goldfields were remarkably free of crime and violence—and McQuestion had no doubt that he would continue to succeed. Steele was a hard-bitten old warhorse: shrewd, blunt, fiercely proud of the Mounted Police and of his country, and as tough as dried moose meat. Even though he was in his fifties and his hair was gray and his mustache white and stiff, he looked as though he was still capable of cleaning out a saloon in a brawl. McQuestion didn't like him; few people did. But he respected him more than most men he'd met.

The colonel looked up from a stack of reports on

his desk and frowned as McQuestion stepped inside. "What are you doing here, Corporal? You're supposed to be on patrol downstream."

McQuestion said, "I finished patrol yesterday, sir, and swung down toward Fort Reliance. It was my intention to spend the night at Molly Malone's roadhouse." He took a breath, released it slowly, and went on to explain how he had found Molly and her two Siwash helpers shot to death. The only facts he omitted from his account were his discoveries of the nankeen scrap and the gold watch fob. The colonel would have asked for both as evidence, and McQuestion was not ready to relinquish them yet.

When he'd finished speaking, Steele's mouth was pinched and his eyes showed outrage. "Sit down, Corporal," he said. And when McQuestion had complied, opening his parka because it was warm in the office: "So you believe they were killed for food and whiskey?"

"Yes, sir, I do," McQuestion said. "Primarily for the food."

"What manner of men would murder a woman for a cache of supplies? This is *not* a starvation camp, by God."

McQuestion remained silent. But he was thinking: Cheechakos, perhaps. Perhaps.

"Were you able to determine which direction the men headed?" Steele asked.

"No, sir. There had been a fresh snowfall just before I arrived; it covered their sled tracks."

"And you found nothing at all that might help identify them?"

"Not a thing. But it was dark and I searched the building by lantern light. I might have overlooked something."

Steele grunted, ran a hand through his gray hair. "I had best have a look myself, then. I can be ready to leave for the roadhouse by noon; that should allow you and your dogs time for food and a short rest."

"You want me to accompany you, sir?"

"Do you object to that?"

"I'd prefer to stay here," McQuestion said.

"Why?"

"It's possible the killers came to Dawson or are from around here. Someone might know something and be willing to talk about it."

"One of the other men can investigate that possibility."

"Yes, sir, but I'd rather be the one to do it. I found the bodies; I would like to actively pursue the investigation myself."

Steele studied him for a moment. "For what reason?"

"Molly Malone was a friend of mine."

"Yes, so I've heard."

Again McQuestion was silent.

"Rumor has it," Steele said, "you were keeping company with her. The clandestine sort. Is that a fact?"

McQuestion said thinly, "If it is, sir, it's my business."

"Not if you were spending nights with her when you were supposed to be on patrol."

"Does rumor have that, too?"

"It does."

"Then rumor lies. I have never skirted my duty, Colonel. Not once."

Steele seemed satisfied with that, at least for the moment. In his blunt way he asked, "Were you in love with the woman?"

"No," McQuestion said.

"Was she in love with you?"

"No. But we liked and understood each other— better than most married people, I expect. She was a good woman and she shouldn't have died as she did. I want the men responsible as badly as I've ever wanted anything."

"Vengeance, Corporal?"

"I won't deny that."

"And if you find the men? What then?"

"I would bring them in to stand trial, of course."

"Unharmed?"

"If possible, yes."

Steele studied him again, even more speculatively this time. At length he asked, "Who are you, McQuestion?"

"I don't know what you mean, sir."

"I mean just that: who are you? Oh, I've read your file—all the facts and figures. Born in Manitoba in '69, Canadian mother and Scotch-American father. Raised in the States . . . the Dakotas, wasn't it?"

"Yes."

"Joined the Mounted Police in '93. Stationed at Athabasca Landing, stationed in Alberta, transferred here sixteen months ago. Exemplary record, except for a tendency to bend regulations when it suits you." Steele paused. "Why that tendency? Do you feel you know better than the manual?"

"No, sir. But justice is the important thing, not strict adherence to any set of regulations. Or so I believe."

"Justice *is* adherence to a set of regulations. But perhaps you have your own ideas of what is just. That Siwash you brought in last fall for burglary. You permitted his brother to slip across the border to Alaska, didn't you? The brother was also at the Indian camp when you arrived to make your arrest, wasn't he?"

McQuestion said carefully, "The brother was innocent of any complicity in the crime, sir."

"So you say."

"He was innocent," McQuestion repeated.

Steele allowed another few seconds of silence to pass before he asked, "Why did you decide to become a Mounted Policeman, McQuestion?"

"I've always been interested in law enforcement, sir. My father was a peace officer."

"Ben McQuestion. A well-known lawman in the Dakotas, I understand."

"He was, yes. He retired seven years ago, after he was shot during a holdup attempt and nearly lost a leg."

"Your idea of justice comes from him, does it?"

"More or less. He taught me to respect the law."

"And that is what led you to join the Force."

"Yes."

"You had no other reasons?"

He had, but McQuestion said, "No, sir."

"Facts and figures don't tell me much about a man," Steele said. "The man himself does that, directly or indirectly. But not you. You haven't told me anything about yourself while we've been talking. You don't discuss your background or your interests or your private feelings with anyone. You have no close friends among the men. So I ask you again: who are you?"

"A man who keeps his own counsel and who prefers his own company most of the time. I have reasons for valuing my privacy."

"Reasons you won't mention?"

"They are personal, sir."

"I see. You'll say no more to answer my question?"

"I've already answered it, sir."

Steele reached for his canister of tobacco and spent several seconds filling a scarred black briar. When he had it packed to his satisfaction he said, "You will report to me immediately if you learn anything relevant to the murders. If at any time you find yourself in a position to arrest the men responsible, you'll do so in proper accordance with regulations and with every effort to forgo violence. Otherwise, I will see to it that your career with the Force is terminated—and if necessary, that you're brought up on charges. Is all of that clear?"

"Yes, sir."

"Good. I should be back from the roadhouse by tomorrow morning at the latest. I will expect a report from you by noon."

"You'll have it, Colonel."

Steele had no more to say. He lit his pipe, stood, caught his parka off a wall peg, and silently accompanied McQuestion outside. The Redcoat McQuestion had spoken to earlier had removed Molly Malone's blanket-wrapped body from the sledge and laid it on a cache—a framework of poles— away from the kennel area. Steele went to examine it. But McQuestion turned aside; he did not want to look again at Molly's dead face.

He left his team chained to one of the kennel

posts and went back up Front Street on foot. His left hand was under his parka, touching the pocket of his scarlet uniform coat where the watch fob and piece of nankeen were.

Somebody had to be able to identify one or the other, he was thinking. Somebody, somewhere, had to know *something* . . .

CHAPTER 3

HIS FIRST STOP was the Alaska Commercial Company's warehouse and general store. But the clerk there, an old-timer who knew most of the sourdoughs and cheechakos in the Yukon Valley, could tell him nothing about the fob. Nor could Father Judge, the Jesuit missionary who had built Dawson's first hospital and church and who also knew most men in the area. Nor could the clerk in the recorder's office. Nor could the tinker or the lawyer or the two barbers who had set up shop in tents sandwiched between the town's more permanent wooden buildings. Nor could the bartenders or hostesses in the first half-dozen saloons and gambling houses. Nor could Swiftwater Bill, Three-Inch White, or any of the other prospectors he spoke to.

By the time McQuestion approached the Frontier Saloon, the better part of two hours had passed and the sun had crept up as high above the bulge of the earth as it would get: not much more than a quarter of its upper rim was visible. The sky was palely lit and shadows still crouched throughout the settlement. The Miners' Cafe seemed huddled alongside the larger saloon building, dark and deserted in the gray light. Like the other cafes, the Miners' had closed its doors before Christmas for lack of supplies.

The snow in front of the Frontier had been beaten down to a glazed sheet by mukluks and snowshoes and sled runners. McQuestion crossed it carefully, entered the saloon. The Frontier had been built the previous summer, by a man from Seattle named Ruckhammer who had come into Dawson with the first wave of stampeders. Ruckhammer ran a rough house; there had been a number of brawls, as well as two complaints of shortchanging on his scales and another that his faro and roulette games were rigged. He was still in business because the Mounted Police hadn't yet been able to prove any of the allegations.

The place wasn't crowded; with the warmer temperatures and no snowfall today, most of the valley's miners were out working their claims. The men lining the plank bar were a quiet, listless lot, a few showing the effects of scurvy—dry skin, gray-

ish pallor, swollen gums, and sunken eyes—and all
with the gaunt, tight-bellied, hungry look of men
who had weathered a hard winter on short rations.
The faro and roulette layouts were getting little
play. None of the men spoke much to one another,
nor did they pay much attention to McQuestion as
he stomped snow from his pacs and stood survey-
ing the room. He hadn't told anyone why he was
asking about the owner of the watch fob. And news
of Molly's murder hadn't yet leaked out of the police barracks.

The Frontier was a far cry from the Dawson saloons before the rush. They all looked the same but
they weren't. Back then, the sourdoughs tossed
their pokes on the bar when they came in, then
turned their backs while the saloonkeeper weighed
out the price in gold dust of a drink or a bottle.
Watching a man weigh your poke was an insult in
those days. The tavern owners had been bankers,
arbiters of disputes, traders of ready cash and provisions for small portions of claims, and friends to
every miner who walked through their doors.

With Ruckhammer's breed of saloonkeeper it
was different. Every sourdough learned to watch
his type squarely as he weighed out dust and
watched his croupiers and dealers, too, to make
sure the games of chance stayed reasonably honest.
And the whiskey he served was far more likely to
be hooch than good American or Canadian bond—

bootleg stuff made of molasses and dried berries, with a wad of sourdough thrown in to hurry the fermentation. Koprecof Dynamite was what Ruckhammer poured, and there wasn't much the Force could or cared to do about it. The last bottle of decent whiskey in Dawson had been drained weeks before.

McQuestion moved to the bar, to where Ruckhammer sat on a stool beside his scales. At the back of the room, the piano player banged out a ragtime tune. It did little to dispel the atmosphere of dispirited lethargy that hung like tobacco smoke in the too-warm air.

Ruckhammer said, "Afternoon, Corporal," in his greasily polite way as McQuestion bellied up to the bar in front of him. He was fat, red-faced, with a thick mustache and great round eyes that reminded McQuestion of a snow owl's. "Drink, will you?"

"No, not today." McQuestion laid the watch fob on the scarred surface of the plank. "I'm looking for the man who owns this fob."

Ruckhammer leaned over to peer at it, then flipped it over with a forefinger. "Floyd," he said. "Floyd who?"

"That's what I want to know."

"Well. Afraid I can't help you."

"Not familiar?"

"No, sir. Never saw it before."

A few of the sourdoughs had overheard and

came crowding around. One of them said, "Say, I seen something looked like that a while back. Sure I did."

McQuestion turned sharply. He knew the man who had spoken—a thin, cadaverous dog-puncher named Charley Upfield, late of the Dyea mail. "Who, Charley? Who owns the fob?"

"Well, I don't exactly know," Upfield said. "Warn't a fob I seen. Little gold-plated horseshoe, it was. Same words on it, though: 'FLOYD' on one side, 'GOOD LUCK' on the other. Fella I played poker with one night had it. Tried to put it in the pot when he run low on dust. Hell. Warn't worth half what he said it was, little thing like that."

"Cheechako, was he?"

"He was. Green as they come."

"Prospector?"

"Claimed to be. Didn't look to me like he could find a pimple on a whore's ass, let alone gold."

Some of the other sourdoughs laughed. Mc-Question asked, "Where was his claim? Did he say?"

"Not so's I recall," Upfield said.

"And you didn't get his full name?"

"He didn't give it. Just Floyd."

"What did he look like?"

"Little booger, top of his head come up to about my chin. Face like a ferret."

"When was this, Charley?"

"Three-four months ago. Maybe longer."

"Where?"

"Right here in the Frontier."

"You come across him anywhere since?"

"Don't believe so, no."

"Was there anybody with him that night?"

"Partner or sidekick, you mean? No."

McQuestion swung his gaze back to Ruckhammer. "You've been listening, Mr. Ruckhammer. Remember this Floyd now?"

"Can't say I do," Ruckhammer said, and shrugged.

"Who else was in the poker game?" McQuestion asked Upfield. "Maybe one of them can tell me about Floyd."

"Maybe, but I kind of doubt it. Deephole Johnson was one; he didn't know Floyd either because he told me so. Fourth hand was Arlo Cashman. You know Arlo? Got a claim out on Hunker Creek. He was the big winner that night. Cleaned the cheechako out inside an hour. Well, almost cleaned him out, I should say. This Floyd left with at least twenty dollars; I recollect him sayin' it." Upfield grinned suddenly. "Why, hell, that's right. He needed the twenty on account of he had him a date."

"He say who the date was with?"

"Yep. Sweet Sue. I reckon old Floyd could find him a pimple on a whore's ass, after all."

The sourdoughs laughed again. McQuestion's long, lean face remained a stoic mask. He said to Ruckhammer, "Pour Charley a drink for me. I'll settle with you later." Then he nodded to the dog-puncher, caught up the watch fob, and hurried out of the Frontier.

He didn't go far: just up the street to Paradise Alley, the short sidestreet where Dawson's bawdy houses were located. The buildings there were all made of whipsawed planks; some were private cabins and some were cribs, and the windows of all were adorned with scarlet curtains. The Force refused to allow the prostitutes to advertise with red lanterns; the curtains served that purpose and one other: Closed, they announced that a lady had company. Open, they invited inspection, negotiation, and a few minutes or a few hours of companionship during the long Arctic days and nights.

The curtains at Sweet Sue's private cabin were open. McQuestion knocked on the door, stood waiting half a minute before it was opened. Sweet Sue blinked in surprise when she saw him. Then one side of her heavily rouged mouth quirked upward and she said, "Well, my, my. Corporal McQuestion, isn't it?"

"It is."

"Don't tell me this is a social call?"

"I'm here on my business, Sue, not yours."

"That is too bad," she said. Her eyes were inso-
lent. "I haven't done anything wrong, have I?"

"Not to my knowledge."

Puzzlement came into Sweet Sue's expression.
The Redcoats rarely bothered Dawson's whores unless they took up drunk-rolling or loading their customers' whiskey with knockout drops. "Well then?"
she asked.

"Can we talk inside?"

"Certainly. Before all the heat rushes out."

He entered the cabin. Both the furnishings and
Sweet Sue's wardrobe were opulent by Dawson
standards. The bed had a brass frame and a down
mattress; a low oil lamp covered with an old-rose
silk shade burned on a table beside it. A marble-
topped lavatory stood against one wall, next to the
sheet-iron stove. An open steamer trunk revealed an
impressive array of clothing: satin dresses, seal-
skins, a white fox capote, two beaver hats. Care-
lessly tossed over a carved Boston rocker were a
pair of marten pelts.

McQuestion was not surprised. Whores always
lived well in rush camps, where the prices for their
favors were high and a few men were usually willing to bestow presents of one kind or another for
extra attention. Rumor had it that Sweet Sue was
the most passionate trollop in the Territory. And she
was a handsome woman to boot, despite her rouged
whore's mask: no more than twenty-five, plump,

heavy-breasted, with hennaed hair cut short. Her silk skirts were cut short too, and she wore black silk stockings and a lacy camisole open at the throat. It was plain she had suffered little or no hardship during the long winter. Among the presents she'd received would have been plenty of food and liquor.

She didn't invite McQuestion to sit down. Instead she began rolling a cigarette, her fingers as deft with the makings as any man's, and asked lazily, "What is it you want with me, Redcoat?"

He showed her the fob, turning it over in his hand so she could see both sides of it. "I'm looking for the man who owns this," he said. "He also owns a gold pocket horseshoe with the same words printed on it. Little gent, ferret-faced—a cheechako."

"What makes you think I know him?"

"You know him, Sue. He spent time with you three or four months ago."

She finished rolling her smoke, struck a lucifer, and held it away from her to let the sulfur burn off. The cigarette danced in one corner of her mouth as she said, "What has he done, this Floyd?"

"Committed murder, I expect. Tell me the rest of his name."

"Murder?" The word made her hand twitch slightly as she lit the cigarette. When she spoke again the coyness and the insolence were both gone from her voice. "Loomis," she said. "Floyd Loomis. But I hardly know him; he only visited me twice. And I've not seen him since before Christmas."

"Where was he living then?"

"I don't exactly know. He said he had a claim on Bonanza Creek—way up near the Dome, not any of the rich ones around Discovery."

"Did he work it alone or with a partner?"

"He didn't say."

"Did you ever see him with another man?"

"No. He always came alone. I don't allow crowds."

"What did he tell you about himself?"

"Hardly anything. Just that he came from Idaho."

"Where in Idaho?"

"Some town I never heard of. Near the Washington border, he said it was."

"What else did he talk about while he was here?"

"He didn't do much talking. Men generally don't have the time or the energy for words when they're visiting Sweet Sue."

McQuestion ignored that. "Is there anything else you can tell me about Loomis?"

"No. He was just a customer, like all the rest." She exhaled smoke through her nostrils, male-fashion. "Who did he murder, anyhow?"

McQuestion ignored that, too. He thanked her curtly and left her still wearing the puzzled look.

Back at the recorder's office, he gave the clerk Floyd Loomis's name and asked him to look up the number of the man's claim on Bonanza Creek. The clerk complied. "Forty-seven Above Discovery," he said. "But Loomis don't own it anymore."

"No? Who does?"

"Fella named Claybaugh—Jeff Claybaugh."

"When did Loomis sell it to him?"

"Back in November, right after the big fire. The twenty-ninth. Claybaugh paid him a hundred dollars for the parcel."

"Did Loomis buy another claim with the money?"

"No, sir. Nor a fraction neither."

"They friends, him and Claybaugh?"

"Not so's you'd notice. Strictly business when they come in here in November." The clerk shook his head. "Cheechakos, both of 'em. Hell, Claybaugh has to be even greener than Loomis to've paid a hundred dollars for a claim that far up the Bonanza. They're all skunks that close to the Dome. Anybody with sense knows that."

McQuestion asked, "You know any of Loomis's friends?"

"Sorry, I don't."

"When did he first file Forty-seven Above?"

"Let's see—May of last year, it was. The eighteenth."

"And he filed it alone? No partner?"

"Just him."

"Did he give an address Outside?"

"No, sir, he sure didn't."

When McQuestion came outdoors again he stood looking up at the cold gray sky. The rim of the sun was still visible; there were a couple of hours of daylight left. No storms in the offing for tonight— no snowfall at all, he thought, until tomorrow morning at the earliest. Twenty below tonight, at the coldest. Not a bad night for camping on the trail if it became necessary.

He nodded once to himself and hurried back down to the police barracks.

CHAPTER 4

THE REDCOATS, LIKE everyone else in the Yukon Valley, were on short rations—so much so that Colonel Steele had issued orders to his men not to arrest anyone for minor offenses unless the person had his own provisions. All McQuestion could get from the barracks mess was some fatty pemmican, bannocks, and a ration of black tea to replenish his dwindling trail supplies.

Out back at the kennels, he found his sledge up on a cache; the constable in charge of the kennels had seen to that, to keep loose dogs from ripping the sled sheet on a hunt for grub. McQuestion lifted the sledge down off the cache, stowed the bannocks, then the pemmican, in his meat can. He turned out his dogs, hitched Takus first and the others in tandem, took his place at the gee-bar, and cracked his whip to start the team.

He drove them out onto the frozen surface of the Klondike, under the long, shaky footbridge that connected Dawson with Lousetown, and mushed them along the well-packed sled road that led straight upriver. It took him half an hour to reach Bonanza Creek, two and a half miles up the Klondike on the river's left bank. Come summer, the creek mouth would be a swampland of mud and weeds; now, with the ice and the winter snowpack, portage was easy enough.

Some distance beyond, the creek forked, with the south fork becoming the Eldorado. At the junction was a miniature Dawson called Grand Forks— one hotel, one saloon, one general store, and two rows of cabins set above each other on the hillside. McQuestion mushed on past the buildings and the men working along the creeks, staying on the Bonanza road and entering the narrowing valley that led to Midnight Dome.

The valley was hazed over with the smoke from hundreds of shaft fires. Even in the summer the ground here was frozen, and the rich pay dirt lay from fourteen to twenty feet under the glacial drift, close to bedrock. The only way for the miners to work their claims was to set fire to heavy logs and burn five-foot-wide holes through the drift. Most of the timber had been cut from the valley's slopes for this purpose, as well as to build cabins and shore up the shafts.

Alternately riding the sledge and trotting along behind it with one mittened hand on the gee-bar, McQuestion began counting the ninety-six-foot claims above Discovery as he passed them. There was not much activity beyond Twenty Above; as the recording clerk had said, most of the claims farther up were either worthless or offered prospectors only a meager living. But there was work in progress at Forty-seven Above. A green-spruce fire blazed near the shaft, sending billows of smoke into the chill air. A crude pole-and-mud cabin bulked up at the rear of the claim, and rising majestically behind it was the Dome, its flanks banked with snow and ice and its top wreathed in mist.

McQuestion swung his team off the trail, brought them to a halt near Forty-seven's snow-flecked gravel dump. He gave the dogs the command to lie down in their traces, then tramped between the dump and the fire to the windlass at the shaft's edge. From there, he could see a lone man working on the bottom, sweeping the bedrock with a broom made of spruce twigs, shoveling the sweepings into a bucket. The man was intent at his work; he didn't look up until McQuestion spoke.

"Mr. Claybaugh? Jeff Claybaugh?"

The face that peered up at him then, still half hidden by the hood of his mackinaw, was young and broad and swarthy, shining with a glaze of sweat. "That's right," the man answered warily. "Who're you?"

"Corporal Zachary McQuestion, North West Mounted Police. I'd like a few words with you, Mr. Claybaugh."

"A Redcoat?" Claybaugh sounded surprised, but not worried or uneasy. "Well, now. I'll be right up."

There was a rough-fashioned ladder leaning against the shored wall of the shaft. Claybaugh climbed it, quick and agile despite his heavy clothing. He and McQuestion stood for a few seconds, assessing each other; then Claybaugh said, "Trouble of some kind? Your face says so."

"Trouble," McQuestion agreed. "I'm looking for Floyd Loomis."

"That so? Well, I haven't seen Loomis since he sold me this claim back in November." Claybaugh grinned; it made him look even younger than he was. "He thought it was a skunk—that's why he let me have it cheap. But he was wrong. About as wrong as a man can be."

McQuestion had heard that before. Sourdoughs always thought their claims were rich, that they were only a few hours or a few days from a vein of pure gold, and cheechakos were the worst of all. He didn't offer a response.

"You mind if I keep on working while we talk?"

Claybaugh asked. "I don't like to waste any daylight."

"Go ahead."

"Thanks." Claybaugh moved to the windlass, began to wind up the bucket full of sweepings.

McQuestion said, "Do you know where Loomis went after you took over here?"

"He said something about throwing in with another prospector on Indian River."

"He tell you the prospector's name?"

"I think he did mention it. Can't recall it offhand; give me a minute."

McQuestion waited. Claybaugh finished hauling up the bucket, dumped the black gravel into a washing pan that sat nearby. A petrol tin stood at the fire's edge; Claybaugh hoisted it out, poured boiling water into the pan, then began to flick off ashes and bits of charcoal that remained from the shaft fire.

"Baxter," he said finally. "No, that's not right . . . Thaxter. Yes, sir, it was Thaxter."

"First name?"

"I don't believe Loomis gave it."

"Did he say where on Indian River this fellow Thaxter's claim was?"

"Not that I can remember."

"Or anything about the man?"

"No."

"You ever meet Thaxter yourself?"

"Never did, no."

"How well do you know Loomis?"

"Hardly at all," Claybaugh said. "Met him in Dawson, at Diamond Tooth Gertie's Saloon. I'd been working for Sam Rollins, out on Hunker Creek, and I told Loomis I was looking to buy a claim of my own. That's when we struck our deal."

Claybaugh had been rocking the pan as he spoke; now he pulled off one of his mittens, began scraping out pieces of gravel. McQuestion could see a few coarse grains of dull yellow metal and one tiny, irregular nugget. But from the way Claybaugh beamed, he might have been looking at a cheese sandwich—the sourdough's term for a big nugget flattened between layers of rock.

"Quarter ounce or more," Claybaugh said. His eyes were bright and hot with the fever. "Five dollars to the pan, at least—that's what I've been washing lately. Come the thaw so I can sluice my dump, I figure I'll double that amount easy. If I don't hit pay dirt in the meantime. And I might, I just might!"

McQuestion left him, went back to his sledge and got the dogs up. Indian River was some fifteen miles from here, back up the Yukon—a good three-hour run overland. He didn't want to take the time to detour into Dawson, and he wouldn't need to in order to find out where Thaxter's claim was located. There was not enough gold along the Indian to attract a large number of miners. The men who did prospect there all knew one another.

Claybaugh was adding more wood to his fire, from a stack of it nearby, when McQuestion mushed his team out onto the sled road. Lost again in his fevered golden dream, the cheechako did not even look up.

It was well past nightfall, the waving banners of the northern lights brightening the sky, when Mc-Question reached the first prospector's cabin on Indian River. It was one of those that had been built by the Hudson's Bay Company during their involvement in the Yukon fur trade; the initials H.B.C. were burned into the front door—initials that, according to those who disliked the almighty attitude of the Company, stood for "Here Before Christ." Now the cabin was occupied by an old Finnish sourdough named Machi. And Machi was home tonight: lamplight glowed dully through the rimed windows, smoke curled out of the stovepipe.

Machi's dogs commenced barking when Mc-Question drew his team up near the cabin. The door opened as he stepped off the runners, and the old Finn stood in the frame of light with a Henry .30-30 carbine in his hands. As isolated as the prospectors out here were, with a mile or two between most of the diggings, they were a cautious lot when it came to unexpected visitors after dark.

"Hell," Machi said when he recognized Mc-Question. "It's you, Corporal." He lowered the rifle. "Ay didn't know what to tink when Ay seen your sledge."

"Everything all right with you, Machi?"

"Ay'm gettin' along. But Ay'll get along better come breakup. She's been hell of a winter, ain't she?"

McQuestion nodded. "Your grub holding out?"

"Yah. But Ay ain't got enough to spare, so Ay can't offer you supper."

"I've already eaten," McQuestion lied.

"Well, come in and warm yourself. Tea, now, Ay got plenty of."

McQuestion settled the dogs and then followed Machi inside the cabin. It was a bare twelve-by-twelve, with a puncheon floor and wimpled, mud-chinked walls. The single bunk was covered with striped Hudson's Bay Company blankets. A hot fire burned in the sheet-iron stove; the remains of a meager supper littered the rough-plank table. Three No. 4 jump traps hung by their chains from a wall peg. Machi had been in the Yukon a long time, long enough for the edge to wear off his gold fever, and he had taken to trapping marten and Arctic fox to supplement his income.

He poured tea into a tin cup while McQuestion took off his mittens, beat frost particles from the fur of his parka. When Machi handed over the cup he

said, "Ay don't tink you come all the way out here
on routine patrol. Not from what Ay see in your
face."

"You're right."

"You hunting somebody?"

"Yes." McQuestion saw no reason to keep the
truth from Machi. He would have to say the words
sooner or later; better to get them said now. "I'm
hunting two murderers. They killed Molly Malone
at her roadhouse last night. Shot her and her two Siwash helpers and stuffed their bodies in the storage
shed out back."

"Good Yesus!" Machi said.

There was a silence. Outside, the wind whistled
at the chinks in the cabin wall and one of the malemutes set up a howl that others answered. McQuestion was aware of the strong gummy odor of the
spruce burning in the sheet-iron stove. The old
Finn's eyes were shocked; like everyone else in the
Territory, he had known and liked Molly. And like
everyone else, he had heard the rumors about her
and McQuestion.

At length Machi sighed and said heavily, "Ay'm
sorry, Corporal. Ay know how you must feel."

No, you don't, McQuestion thought. But he said,
"It looks to've been two men after food. The storeroom was cleaned out."

"Who would do such a ting for grub?"

"I'm not sure yet. But one of them may be a cheechako named Floyd Loomis."

The old Finn's mouth worked as if he wanted to spit. He said something sharp in his native language.

"You know him, then," McQuestion said.

"Ay met him couple of times. He come by after grub one night. Ay told him Ay couldn't spare none, and he try to take some pemmican. He tink Machi is weak old man; Ay showed him he was plenty wrong. He never come try again, that's for sure."

"He works for a man named Thaxter, doesn't he?"

"William Thaxter, yah. But you don't find him on Thaxter's claim."

"No? Why not?"

"Nobody there now. They abandon that claim two months back."

"You know where they went?"

"Ay couldn't tell you. One day they're working, next day they're gone. They don't tell nobody nothing. And they don't come back."

"Why do you think they left?"

"That claim is skunk, that's why. Everybody knows that except cheechakos."

"Thaxter's a cheechako, too?"

"Sure. He come out here last fall, yust after he arrive in the Yukon."

"Was Loomis with him then?"

"No. Loomis don't come until December."

"So Thaxter was alone up to that time?"

"Well, he wasn't alone when he come, no. He had woman with him. Indian woman—half-breed. But she don't stay long."

"Something happen to make her leave?"

Machi shrugged. "One morning Ay see her come down the river ice, she got a full pack strapped on and she don't look too happy. She goes right by me, she don't even turn her head. That's the last Ay see of her."

"You know her name?"

"Yah. Thaxter called her Kate."

"Just Kate? No other name?"

"He don't tell me no other one."

"Any idea where he hooked up with her?"

"Ay couldn't even guess."

McQuestion drank some of the strong black tea. "Tell me about Thaxter. What kind of man is he?"

"Ay didn't like him worth a damn," Machi said. "He got big mouth, always bragging how he gets rich someday and buys fancy tings, goes fancy places, and to hell with everybody. He got mean streak, too. One-Ear Muller seen him beating one of his dogs with tree branch. Damn near kill that poor dog yust because it steal little piece of meat. Ay guess it don't surprise me none he'd kill woman for grub."

"I don't know yet that he did," McQuestion said. "I won't know until I catch up to him and Loomis."

"But you tink it's them two. How come?"

McQuestion told him about the watch fob and the piece of nankeen. Machi nodded. "Yah," he said, "that Loomis he wears nankeen trousers. Ay seen it with my own eyes."

"What does Thaxter look like?"

"Big man, pretty near twice so big as Loomis. Got red hair and red beard." Machi snorted. "Only damn-fool cheechako lets his beard grow in Yukon winter."

"He ever talk about where he came from?" McQuestion asked.

"Ay tink he come from California, but Ay don't know yust where."

"How far is his claim from here?"

"About five mile. Yust above Cranberry Creek. You know where that is, yah?"

McQuestion nodded. "Anybody living there now?"

"Nobody. Not since Thaxter and Loomis abandon it."

"I'd better take a run up there," McQuestion said. He finished his tea, set the empty cup on the table. "But I'm not carrying a lantern, Machi; I'll need to borrow one of yours."

"Sure ting. You want company, maybe? Ay don't mind a little exercise tonight . . ."

"No. I have to see this through alone."

"Yah," the old Finn said gravely. "Ay understand."

He got the spare lantern, made sure there was oil in the fount, and passed it over. McQuestion said he would return it later that night or first thing in the morning. Then he turned for the door.

Machi followed him. "What you going to do when you catch up with them two? You going to shoot them like they shoot Molly?"

"No," McQuestion said, "I'm going to arrest them and bring them in to stand trial."

And maybe that's a lie. Maybe I'll shoot both of them dead the minute I lay eyes on them . . .

CHAPTER 5

THE CABIN ON Cranberry Creek had been crudely and poorly built. McQuestion could tell that even before he reached it, because it sat on a hummock and was clearly outlined in the bright, colored flickers of the northern lights. The front wall had begun to lean, and between the unevenly notched logs were gaps the size of a man's fist where the mud chinking had fallen or been blown out. It was typical of cabins built all over the Territory by cheechakos with little or no bush experience.

He took the dogs over to the lee side, settled them, then caught up the lantern Machi had loaned him and went around to the front. The door was still latched but loose in its frame; the single window in front had been covered with a sheet made of flattened tin cans. Inside, snow that had been whirled in through the gaps lay drifted on the floor. Mc-Question wedged the door shut, leaned back against it. He managed to get the lantern lighted by shielding it with his body from the incoming drafts of icy wind.

Thaxter and Loomis had left little enough behind when they cleared out. The only remaining furniture were two rough bunks, a collapsed table, two benches, and a caved-in woodbox. McQuestion moved around the walls, holding the lantern up in front of him. The logs were all bare, although nails and pegs showed where things had once been hung.

The drifted snow on the floor was six inches to a foot deep. McQuestion scuffed through it in a series of swaths from front to back without turning up anything more than a broken pick, an empty laudanum bottle, and an empty sack that had once contained salt. He was at the rear wall, about to give up the search, when the light picked up a scrap of stiff paper half buried in the snow he'd just kicked into the corner.

He sat on his heels and lifted the scrap, held it in front of the lantern. It was half of a jaggedly torn photograph, the grainy outdoor kind taken by itinerant photographers during the summer months. It showed an attractive young breed Indian woman dressed in buckskins, smiling in a tentative way at the camera; part of a man's arm was also visible at the torn edge. But it was the background that most interested McQuestion: an Indian village, pole houses with roofs covered with moss. The village had a familiar look. If the other half of the photograph was also here somewhere . . .

He dragged one of the benches over, set the lantern on it, and began to sift through the snow in that corner. It took him five minutes to find the second torn piece. Reckoning from Machi's description, the man in it was William Thaxter. McQuestion studied the image for several seconds. Then, when the face was burned into his mind, he fitted the two halves together and gave his attention to the village in the background.

Less than a minute later he stood, carefully stowed the torn photograph inside his parka, and blew out the lantern. The village was the one at Caribou Crossing. There was no doubt of it in his mind; he'd been there often enough to recognize the arrangement of houses.

McQuestion made camp a mile from the cabin, in the lee of a thick spruce scrub fifty yards off the river ice. Atop a bank nearby, he found a high-water deposit of dry firewood and went to work on it with his trail ax. When he had a fire built he pitched a fly with his sled sheet between two of the trees. Then he unharnessed the dogs, fed and watered them, got them bedded down. He still had no appetite; he had to force himself to eat a bannock and some pemmican with his billycan of tea.

Propped on the spruce boughs he'd laid in the shelter, tucked up under his buffalo robe, he filled and lit the stubby pipe he carried. And smoked and watched the northlights sputter and die. The sky turned as black as India ink; the stars were like crystals of ice imbedded in it—as cold and sharp and bright as any he had ever seen. The moon that had risen was lopsided and a quarter beyond full, with a halo encircling it that presaged another storm for tomorrow.

Around him, the night wind made humming, murmuring sounds like snatches of a song heard from far away. And another, familiar song, sweet and haunting, began to hum and murmur in his memory.

> *In Scarlet town, where I was born,*
> *There was a fair maid dwellin',*
> *Made every youth cry "Well-a-way!"*
> *Her name was Barbara Allen.*

Molly's favorite song. She had sung it for him many times when they were alone, plucking out the chords on her guitar, her voice strong and lilting. A fine voice. She had flushed with pleasure the first time he told her that. "It's the only gift God gave me besides the ability to run a roadhouse," she'd said. He had asked her then why she favored "Barbara Allen," and she'd said, "I feel a kinship with her. I've had the same luck with the men in my life—the very same."

All in the merry month of May
When green buds they were swellin',
Young Jemmy Grove on his death-bed lay,
For love of Barbara Allen.

She had been married once, in Portland, Oregon, to an Irish politician named James Malone; he had been killed in a freak dray accident on his way home with a present for Molly's birthday. After the funeral she had packed her belongings and set out for new territory and a new life. In Spokane, Washington, she had met a lawyer, Ben Slattery, and they had been engaged to be married. But Slattery came down with influenza and died two weeks before the wedding.

She had packed and moved on again, to Juneau, Alaska, near where she'd opened her first roadhouse. When news of the Yukon strike came she had sold that place, packed her things yet again, and traveled to Dawson. In the three years since the death of Ben Slattery, she had allowed no man in her life. But loneliness is a powerful emotion, as McQuestion himself well knew; a kinship had developed between them, a bond against the long, empty nights, and when the need in both of them became great, they had become lovers as well as friends.

Still, as he'd told Colonel Steele, what they shared had not been love in the conventional sense. Nor was there any permanency in their relationship. Molly had told him more than once that she would never marry again, never allow herself to fall in love again. She had lost two men—she would not lose a third.

McQuestion understood. He had lost someone he loved, too, back in the States. There would be no marriage for him either. No one could or would take Eileen's place.

Eileen. The town beauty—fine brown hair that shone red in the sun, gentle brown eyes asparkle with laughter. Eighteen to his twenty-one that day they had stood together on the train platform in Bismarck, just before he left for Harvard, the Eastern college where his father had arranged for him to study law. Clutching his arm that day, her body close to his, and her voice promising to wait for him, to be his wife when he returned. Standing there waving, up on tiptoes, as the train pulled out of the station—the last he had ever seen of Eileen, the one image of her that would stay with him until he drew his last breath.

He had been at Harvard six months when her letters stopped coming. Two months after that his father had written him that Eileen had run off with a stockbroker's agent named George Blanton, at least ten years her senior; first been seduced by him, rumor had it. Shattered, McQuestion had left college immediately and come home, and when he arrived his father told him Blanton wasn't a stockbroker's agent after all but a swindler: the stocks Blanton had sold in Bismarck had turned out to be phony. Both his whereabouts and Eileen's were still unknown at that point.

McQuestion, needing time to recover, decided not to resume his college studies right away. So he had still been in Bismarck when word came to Eileen's family, from a town in Colorado, that Eileen had died in childbirth. Died alone, abandoned by George Blanton as soon as he learned she was pregnant, too full of shame to return to her family.

Something had died in McQuestion that day. And something else had been born: a burning hatred for Blanton, an equally burning desire to see the man punished for what he had done to Eileen. "I'll find him!" he'd vowed. And he had gone to the Colorado town and from there spent six long months following a cold trail that had finally heated up as it led him across the border into Saskatchewan. He'd entered a town called Moose Jaw expecting to find Blanton there, astride one of the big grulla horses he favored or swaggering along afoot; instead he had found a grave marker in a hillside cemetery with Blanton's name on it. The man had been discovered dead by the side of the road the week before, McQuestion learned, murdered by an accomplice in a land swindle. The local constable, the undertaker, and half a dozen townspeople all confirmed it: the lightning-fork scar on Blanton's neck left no margin for error.

There had been an emptiness in McQuestion after that, one that could not be filled by returning to college and resuming his law studies. The justice he was interested in now was the kind his father had practiced for twenty years in lawless Dakotas boomtowns, the immediate kind, not the sort that ground exceeding slow and fine in courts of law. He had not been able to make George Blanton answer for his crimes, but there were others of the same ilk he *could* deal with himself. When his decision was made he had traveled from Moose Jaw to Ottawa and by virtue of his Canadian birthright, joined the North West Mounted Police.

But it was justice he was dedicated to, not the Force. The Force was simply a means to that end. This was why he bent regulations; this was why he acted as he felt was necessary, not as he was bound by a set of cold rules and regulations. It was this, too, coupled with the loss of Eileen, that made him a private man, and a lonely one.

Until he told Molly these things, he had shared

the story of his past with no one. The words hadn't come easy, but because it was Molly he was saying them to, and because he had known she would understand, he'd managed to get them said. Later that night, in her bed, she had held him close, saying, "Our lives are so much alike, Zack. Full of tragedy—the people we love dying young while we go on. But *do* we go on, Zack? Or do we die young, too, to make the tragedy complete?"

> *O mother, mother, make my bed,*
> *O make it soft and narrow:*
> *My love has died for me today,*
> *I'll die for him tomorrow.*

And now she was dead, dead young as she had feared; the tragedy of Molly Malone was complete. Maybe he, too, would die young—maybe his days were numbered and soon the tragedy of Zachary McQuestion would also be complete. But not just yet. Not before he found the men who had murdered Molly. Not before he himself saw justice done this time . . .

The tobacco in his pipe had burned out. He tamped out the dottle, sat up to stow the pipe and to hook more wood onto the fire. Somewhere nearby, a snow owl hooted querulously. The only other sound to disturb the night hush was the constant voice of the wind.

He stretched out again, tried to close down his thoughts so he could sleep. But the wind kept singing, singing . . . and another song rose out of his memory, another favorite of Molly's. Much different than "Barbara Allen"—lusty, sardonic, dark-humored. "The Ballad of Sam Hall," an outlaw who was being hanged for murder. One of the verses seemed to swell inside McQuestion's head, repeating itself over and over.

> *Now up the rope I go, up I go;*
> *Yes, up the rope I go, up I go;*
> *And those bastards down below, they'll say*
>   *"Sam, we told you so,"*
> *They'll say, "Sam, we told you so," God*
>   *damn their eyes.*

The bastards who killed Molly, he thought—God damn their eyes!

CHAPTER 6

THE TEMPERATURE DROPPED sharply during the night. At dawn, when he broke camp, McQuestion judged it to be twenty-five below and still dropping. The sky was a dull leaden gray, heavy with boiling cloud masses; you could smell the storm brewing up there.

It began to snow just after he reached the confluence of the Indian and the Yukon. By the time he neared Dawson, the fall was near blinding and he and the dogs were covered from head to foot with ice crystals. His snow goggles kept the wind-whipped flakes from blinding him, but the exposed portions of his face grew numb and lacerated. The blow was the first bad one in more than a week—and it gave warning that the long, hard winter was not yet finished.

When he finally reached the Indian camp at Caribou Crossing, on the other side of Dawson, the snowfall had eased and the shrieking wind had died down enough so that he could hear the crackling of ice under the sledge's runners. But the lull was only momentary. The look of the sky, the feel of the wind, told him the storm would last through the day, perhaps into tomorrow.

The village was small, no more than two dozen houses. With timber being scarce in this area, the houses had been built of small poles laid one on top of the other, notched together like those of a log house and made into double walls some eighteen inches apart. The space in between had been tightly packed with moss. Mossy earth covered the flat roofs as well, except for the smoke hole cut in the middle of each.

Smoke came from several houses, shredded almost instantly by the wind, but McQuestion saw no one outside except three malemutes roughhousing one another. He veered his outfit toward the nearest of the houses, stopped in front of the door, and removed his goggles. As he was rubbing the ice from his face, a man came out of the house and stood looking at him without expression, his breath making great plumes around his head. Like most Tagish men, he was well-set-up and wore a wispy, drooping, Oriental-style mustache. There was a yellowish cast to his red-brown skin that made it look dusky.

"Klahowyam," McQuestion greeted him in the old Chinook jargon.

"Klahowyam, boston."

"Kumtux mika boston wawa?"

"English, yes, I speak," the man said, and nodded his head proudly. Most of the Tagish were easygoing and inclined to be trusting of white men.

McQuestion said, "I'm a Redcoat," and opened his parka to give the man a brief glimpse of his scarlet tunic. "I want to talk to a squaw called Kate. Is she in the village?"

"Kate?" the man said blankly.

McQuestion showed him the torn half of the photograph depicting the breed woman. The man squinted at it, then smiled and nodded again and said, "Kayishtik, she."

"Is Kayishtik here?"

"Yes, *boston.* I take you."

He went back inside briefly, reappeared wearing a twill mackinaw and a pair of snowshoes, and set off. McQuestion followed, riding the sledge. At one of the houses in the middle of the village, the man stopped and pointed. "Kayishtik," he said.

The woman who opened the door at McQuestion's knock was the one in the photograph. She was in her mid-twenties, he judged, with large dark eyes, a broad forehead, prominent cheekbones. Under the woven Chilkat blanket robe she wore, her body seemed willowy and strong.

McQuestion said, "*Klahowyam. Kumtux mika—*"

"Yes, I speak English," she said, without much accent. "I have been to the school at Fort Yukon."

He introduced himself. "May I come in and talk with you, Kayishtik?"

She allowed him to enter. The house was unfurnished except for a platform along one wall that contained supplies and cookware. Rolled blankets on the floor served as bedding. On another blanket near the fire, an old woman sat cross-legged, sewing a twill garment with a bone needle and root fibers for thread; she did not look up at McQuestion. The room smelled of cooked fat, burning spruce, and unwashed bodies—the typical smells of a Tagish house.

Kayishtik invited McQuestion to warm himself at the fire and offered him bark tea, both of which he accepted. He had to step around the old woman to get near the blazing logs, and Kayishtik said, "This is my mother. My father was a white man. He went away when he learned she was to have me."

"Some white men are bad men, Kayishtik."

"Yes. But it was long ago."

"I've come about another white man who may be bad," McQuestion said. "William Thaxter."

Kayishtik stiffened. The emotion that flashed in her dark eyes was unmistakable: bright, cold hatred. "Him," she said, as if the word were an epithet. "That one."

The old woman had finally looked up at the mention of Thaxter's name. In a cracked voice she said, *"Kwass kultus tah!"* and then made a hissing sound like an angry cat.

"My mother says he is an evil spirit, William Thaxter," Kayishtik said. "Perhaps she is right. I know he is an evil man."

"How do you know this?"

"I was his woman for half one year. I know."

"Did he treat you badly?"

"Yes. He beat me with his hands and with sticks."

"Why did he beat you?"

"He is *kultus*. Bad. Evil. It gave him pleasure to hurt me because I am a woman."

"Does he hate all women?"

"It is what I believe. He was kind to me at first. The day he came, on the flat boat as I took fish from the river, he said many kind things. He called me Kate because he could not pronounce my name, and he placed much laughter in my heart. It was only later, when I went with him to Indian River, that the laughter died."

No wonder she hated Thaxter. McQuestion could feel the hatred growing in him, too, for this man he had never met. Woman-beater, misogynist—from these, it was only a small step across a slim line to a woman-killer.

He asked, "You returned to the village when you left Thaxter at Indian River?"

"Yes."

"Did he come after you, try to bring you back?"

"No. He had tired of me, except as a thing to hurt—and there are many things to hurt. I took nothing of his; he had no reason to come after me, William Thaxter. I would not have returned with him if he had. My people would not have permitted him to hurt me again."

"Have you seen him since you left his cabin?"

"No."

"Have you heard anything of him?"

"No. No one here speaks his name."

"When you were living with Thaxter, did a man named Floyd Loomis come to see him?"

Her mouth twisted. "Also *kultus boston*, that one. Yellow eyes, the eyes of a wolf. They devour the spirit as well as the body."

"Did he come often?"

"Two times. William Thaxter gave me to him both times, to do with as he pleased. The first time I refused and he beat me. The second time I did not refuse. It was a source of much laughter for them."

A vein throbbed in McQuestion's neck. He glanced at the old woman, but her head was bowed again and her hands were busy with her needle-work. It was plain she did not understand English.

He said thinly, "Did anyone else visit Thaxter at Indian River?"

"The other prospectors living there," Kayishtik said. "But never more than once did any man come."

"No other friends of Thaxter's, then?"

"William Thaxter has no other friends."

"Did he tell you much about himself? Where he came from? What he did before he traveled to the Yukon?"

"Only at first he spoke of himself. He came from the place called California, William Thaxter—a large village near the one with the name San Francisco."

"Do you remember the name of this village?"

"He spoke it, but I have forgotten."

"Try to remember, Kayishtik."

She tried. And after a time she said, "Oak-land. Yes, it was Oak-land."

"What did he do in Oakland to earn money?"

"He took things from beds in the water."

"Beds in the water?"

"The fish in a shell that lives in such beds."

"Oysters? Oyster beds?"

"Yes. From the boat of his brother."

"Does the brother still live in Oakland?"

"He said yes, William Thaxter."

"What is the brother's first name?"

"I do not know."

McQuestion asked, "Did Thaxter earn much money from his claim at Indian River? Did he find much gold?"

"No. There is not much gold in the earth there. But he did not care. It was the other place he believed had much gold."

"What other place?"

"Two-Willow Creek," she said.

"You mean he had another claim at Two-Willow Creek?"

"No claim. He is afraid to have a claim. Afraid others will come and take it from him."

"What makes him believe there is gold at Two-Willow Creek?"

"I do not know," Kayishtik said. "But he believes it very much, William Thaxter."

"Did he find much there?"

"No. Only on Indian River."

"But not much there either, did he?"

"No. Only enough to buy supplies."

"So he divided his time between the two places?"

Kayishtik nodded. "One week he would stay at Indian River, one week he would go to Two-Willow Creek. Three times he took me with him; after then he would go alone."

"Does he have a cabin at Two-Willow Creek?"

"Yes. Old cabin, Hudson's Bay Company."

"Where, Kayishtik? How far up the creek?"

"Not far. Half one mile."

The muscles across McQuestion's back and shoulders were as tight as drawn bowstrings. The vein in his neck throbbed in a rapid, irregular tempo. Thaxter and Loomis were the ones who had murdered Molly; he was certain of it now. And he was close to finding them, confronting them—close to the hour of reckoning.

Two-Willow Creek flowed into the Chandindu River less than a dozen miles from Molly Malone's roadhouse.

CHAPTER 7

IT WAS MIDAFTERNOON when McQuestion reached the Chandindu River. Most of the run from Caribou Crossing had been through heavy snow flurries and freezing wind, so that he was caked again with ice and the jowls and muzzles of the dogs were whitened by their crystallized breaths. The snowfall was still thick now, but the wind had died some and the flakes slanted down almost vertically instead of being driven on a swirling horizontal plane.

He bypassed the roadhouse, cutting across frozen muskeg below it and out of its sight, picking up the Chandindu just above its mouth. It was doubtful that Colonel Steele was still at the roadhouse this late in the day, but McQuestion did not want to chance meeting him or anyone else from division headquarters. Bringing Thaxter and Loomis in to stand trial—if that was the way it was to work out—was something he *had* to do alone.

For part of the trek up the Chandindu, he was able to travel the river ice. But in places the ice was thin, and in others it had already broken up and there were stretches of open water; when he came on those places he veered off and blazed trail through the heavy land drifts. The river ice was particularly treacherous during the last mile or so below Two-Willow Creek. The previous winter, during an early March thaw, a pair of prospectors from Siwash Creek had broken through and drowned, and their bodies hadn't been recovered until a month after breakup. McQuestion left the river altogether there and mushed overland the rest of the way to Two-Willow Creek.

More danger presented itself when he reached the creek mouth: ice traps. Underground streams flowed down from the rolling hillsides here, ran along under the drift. Except for thin skins of ice, these streams never froze no matter how cold it got. The hidden ice skins would not support a man's weight, let alone that of a sledge—and when the temperature was down to thirty below, as McQuestion judged it was now, plunging ankle or knee-deep into a frigid Arctic stream could be deadly.

He spotted the traps in time to avoid them: the snow above the concealed streams had a sunken, rippled look. He swung the team further inland, past a stand of leafless aspens and up the incline to one of the ice-rimmed ridges that paralleled the watercourse. From there, through the fluttery curtain of snow, he could see some distance along the creek. Black smoke streaked the white-and-gray tableau ahead—the kind of thick, heavy smoke that meant a shaft fire. The cabin Kayishtik had told him about couldn't be seen from this vantage point.

Breaking trail with his snowshoes, the dogs straining against their collars, McQuestion set a slow, cautious pace across two more low hills. When he crested a fourth he saw the cabin. It was set tight against perpendicular rimrock rising from a thick cluster of spruce, fronted by a barren snowfield. In the waning light, the willows that marked the path of the creek were visible more than a hundred yards to the north. McQuestion couldn't see the diggings, but the black smoke told him where they were: behind the spruce-fringed brow of another hill.

Smoke came from the cabin's stovepipe, too, wind-snatched instantly and flung away with the swirling snow. One man in the cabin, McQuestion thought, the other one working the shaft. That was just as well. It would be easier to take them one at a time, as long as he could maintain the element of surprise.

He studied the cabin. Because it had been built by the Hudson's Bay Company, it had a window in front; but the glass was heavily rimed. A man couldn't see out unless he stood up next to it, and then he would have to be looking for something to pick it out through the snowfall. And neither Thaxter nor Loomis should be expecting company.

McQuestion turned the dogs laterally along the slope and a ways below the crown, and left them in the shelter of a rock shelf. He snowshoed back up to where another outcropping, prickly with icicles, gave him cover and an unobstructed view of the cabin. For ten minutes he stood watching through the snowfall, as the sky darkened and night shadows began to gather. Smoke continued to come from the stovepipe; smoke continued to streak the sky from the hidden diggings on Two-Willow Creek. To one side of the building that served as an animal shelter he could see a single sled up on a cache. Another cache, this one larger and higher, made of sturdier poles, had been built alongside the cabin; on it were snow-covered mounds of what McQuestion took to be frozen slabs of bacon and moose meat. He knew where the meat had come from and the knowledge fired his blood and warmed him.

No one came out of the cabin. No one approached it.

Satisfied, he left the outcropping and went down the incline, moving in an awkward run on his snowshoes. He looped around to his right, away from the side of the cabin the window was on, away from the outbuilding so the dogs wouldn't hear him or pick up his scent and start a commotion. He gained the cluster of spruce, cut through the trees to the cabin's side wall. Then he edged around to the front, leaned down next to the door to slip off his snowshoes. The cry of the wind covered what small sounds he made.

He took off his mittens, drew his revolver, and reached out for the door latch. If the door was barred inside, he would have to provoke the dogs so as to bring the man in there outside. But it wasn't barred; he felt the wind shove it inward in his hand. He let go of the latch and rushed inside, crouching, the revolver extended, as the wind slammed the door against the inner wall.

The cabin's lone occupant was at the stove, frying bacon in a skillet; the room was filled with the rich odor of the meat. The man wheeled around, his eyes bulging with surprise and sudden fright. A small man, ferret-faced—Floyd Loomis. The skillet slipped out of his hand and banged to the floor. Strips of bacon flew out, grease spattered the legs of his trousers. Nankeen trousers, with a patch on one knee where a piece of the cloth had been ripped off.

Loomis lunged back and to one side, but it was only a reflex movement to escape the hot grease; there was no fight in him. He put his hands up in from of his chest, palms outward, staring at Mc-Question's pistol. "Who're you?" he said in a reedy voice. "What do you want?"

"You, Loomis. You and your friend Thaxter. For the murder of Molly Malone and her two helpers."

"Redcoat!" The words came out of him in a terrified little gasp.

McQuestion said, "That's right. Corporal Zachary McQuestion, North West Mounted Police." He backed up to the door, caught hold of it with his free hand, brought it around and shouldered it shut to cut off the icy blast of the wind. The snow that had blown in during the few seconds the door had been open lay sifted across the floor like the spilled flour in Molly's storeroom. "You're under arrest, Loomis. Anything you say may be used against you at your trial."

As he spoke, McQuestion let his gaze sweep the cabin. Two bunks made of rawhide-lashed poles, with balsam mattresses and fringed Indian robes. Rough-plank table and benches. Overflowing woodbox, bundles of willow-brush kindling. Wide, braced platform stacked with the stolen supplies. The only weapons he saw were a butcher knife and a Winchester rifle, the rifle leaning against the wall next to the platform.

"I never done it!" Loomis said. It was like hearing the whine of a trapped animal. "I never shot any of 'em, you got to believe me. It was Thaxter—I swear to God, it was Thaxter!"

McQuestion gave the man his full attention. Loomis was sweating: his face looked as if it had been smeared with melted lard. The fear in his eyes was abject. Coward, McQuestion thought. He knew the type: mean, swaggering, cocksure—until trouble came and he found himself under the gun. Then the true nature of him came leaking out of his pores.

"Why did Thaxter shoot the woman?"

"He went crazy," Loomis said. "She didn't want to give us any supplies. That's all we went there after—just a few supplies. We wasn't going to steal 'em. But she wouldn't give us any more credit. Hell, we was starving out here; we hadn't et but a few beans in two days. We'd come back here without grub, we'd of starved to death."

"What happened?"

"She called them Indians of hers to throw us out. That was when Thaxter went off his head. He shot both of 'em. Then the woman, she tried to run out and he—"

"That's enough," McQuestion said flatly.

"I tried to stop him, I swear I did. But he's twice

as big as me and he was wild. There just wasn't nothing I could do. I never wanted no part of murder—"

"I said that's enough!"

Loomis shut up. McQuestion watched him, feeling the hatred, tasting it like metal on the back of his tongue. The man was a liar as well as a coward. Molly would never have turned away two starving men just because they had used up their credit; there was more to what had happened at the roadhouse. Attempted rape, maybe. From what he knew of Thaxter and Loomis, it was as likely that as anything else.

He said, "Turn around, Loomis. Face the wall."

"What for?"

"Turn around, damn you!"

Loomis turned around, his head twisted so he could stare over his shoulder. McQuestion stood unmoving for another few seconds; then, slowly, he relaxed his grip on the pistol. He could not shoot a man down in cold blood, not now and not ever. The part of him that sought justice above all else would always prevent it. To arrest them, to conduct them to Dawson and see them imprisoned—that was retribution enough for any man to extract on his own. It was up to the Crown and the Queen's official hangman to take their lives.

He opened his parka, unhooked the handcuffs from his belt. Then he moved over behind Loomis and prodded him with the revolver. "Hands behind you," he said. "Stretch 'em out."

The little man obeyed. McQuestion snapped the handcuffs over his wrists, then caught his shoulder and turned him and shoved him down the wall until he was sitting on the floor with his legs splayed out in front of him.

"When is Thaxter due back from the diggings?" McQuestion asked as he holstered his weapon.

"No partic'lar time. Sometimes he stays out there half the night. He's got the fever bad."

"You've been out working with him today, haven't you?"

"Yeah. Most of the day since dawn."

"Why'd you come back here?"

"I was hungry." Some of the man's fear had given way to sullenness. "Christ, Redcoat, ain't you ever been hungry in your life?"

"Not hungry enough to kill for grub."

"I told you, I never killed nobody!"

McQuestion let it go. "Is Thaxter expecting you to take him anything to eat?"

"No. He et around noon. He won't want grub again until late."

"So it might be hours yet before he comes in."

"Might be."

"You'd better not be lying to me, Loomis."

"I ain't lying. I'll help you all you want. I don't owe Thaxter nothing, not after what he done."

McQuestion moved to the supply platform. He broke open the rifle, removed the shells, dropped them into one of his pockets. The rest of the supplies yielded a box of spare cartridges for the Winchester, but no other weapon.

He asked Loomis, "Is Thaxter armed?"

"Forty-five sidearm and a Sharps rifle."

Which meant extra caution when he went after the man. And he would have to go after Thaxter, out there at the diggings; there was too much tension involved in waiting here for what might be a long time, too much chance of being caught off guard. Outside, at least, he would have the advantage of stalking his prey.

In one corner of the platform he found a coil of new rope. He cut off a length with the butcher knife, used it to bind Loomis's feet. When he was finished he said, "I'm going out now. If you know what's good for you, you'll be sitting in this same position when I get back."

"I couldn't move if I wanted to, Redcoat," Loomis said. "I'm finished."

Carrying the knife and the box of spare cartridges, McQuestion opened the door and eased his head out. Dusk had settled; the hills and trees were wrapped in shadow. The snowfall had slackened to a light dusting. Over at Two-Willow Creek the black smoke still rose visibly from the shaft fire.

Nothing moved anywhere that he could see on the open snowfields.

He stepped out, shut the door. He buried the knife and the cartridges in the snow, then donned his mittens, strapped on his snowshoes, and moved back into the spruce and along the rimrock toward the creek. The malemutes in the shelter started a soft ruckus as he passed, but the wind was still up: its keening would keep the noise from carrying as far as the diggings.

The spruce thinned out partway along the base of the hill that hid the diggings, so that he had to cross thirty or forty yards of open terrain. But there was no moon yet, and it was faster that way than trying to climb the hill to gain a vantage point. He took his right mitten off, to free that hand, and then drew his revolver and slid both it and the bare hand inside his parka to keep the icy wind from numbing his fingers. As quickly as his footgear would allow, he skirted the base of the hill.

Rocks and scrub brush littered the ground between the hill and the willow-lined creek. Bent low, he ran to the largest of the rocks—a man-sized boulder sheathed with snow and ice. From behind it he was finally able to see the diggings. Thaxter had sunk at least three shafts along the creek bank, the nearest of them some fifty yards distant; the dumps from all three humped up behind them in whitened silhouette, like Indian burial mounds. It was at the nearest one that the fire blazed, its flames staining the evening sky and the snow around it a flickering reddish hue.

There was no sign of Thaxter. But the rope from the windlass trailed down inside the near shaft: he must be working below.

McQuestion scanned the surrounding area, saw nothing moving except the firelight and the wind-torn column of smoke, and edged out from behind the boulder. The wind's voice, as it had at the cabin, covered the crackling, sliding sounds of his snow-shoes as he advanced.

The dump loomed ahead of him. He went around it, across ten yards of open space. The fire snapped and roared twenty paces away on his right; he could feel its warmth as he uncovered his revolver, eased up to the windlass. He leaned forward to peer down inside the shaft.

It was empty.

He spun around, crouching, getting ready to run, cursing himself for being a damned fool. *Ambush!* The wind seemed to shriek the word at him. Thax-ter must have been in a position to see him earlier, as he approached the cabin; must have hidden him-self somewhere nearby . . .

Before he had taken two steps, the first bullet slashed the air over his left shoulder. An instant later, the crack of the rifle echoed and reechoed among the frozen hills. McQuestion flung himself

to his right, away from the spruce fire—the damned
fire that he had blundered right up to and that made
him a clear target. Lost his balance and sprawled
out sideways in the snow seconds before the rifle
cracked a second time. But the fall saved his life.
The bullet sang past above him, slapped into the
snow two feet behind his head.

He rolled over, kicked up puffs of loose snow as
he regained his feet. Thaxter was up on the nearby
hill, hidden among the spruce along its shoulder;
there was no way McQuestion could stand and
fight. His revolver was useless at this distance, in
the semidarkness, and he had no cover: the dump
wasn't high enough or perpendicular enough for
concealment. He started to run back the way he'd
come, toward the man-sized boulder.

The rifle cracked a third time. Seconds later, as
the echoes rolled away, he felt a lash of fiery pain
under his right ear, and in the next instant he was
down in the snow again, his thoughts jarred awry
and the echo of the fourth shot loud inside his head,
like the roar of river ice breaking up in the May
thaw. Particles of snow stung his eyes, filled his
mouth, caked in his nostrils. His lungs felt con-
stricted, frozen.

He struggled up, spitting, gasping for breath. Got
his knees under him and pawed at his eyes with
both hands: he'd lost his revolver. The right side of

his head seemed to have gone numb. He tried to stand, couldn't lift himself up.

The numbness was spreading; he didn't feel anything when the rifle boomed once more, only dimly heard it. Then he was lying on his back, staring up at the bright, icy pattern of the stars. And then the stars were gone and there was nothing but blackness.

CHAPTER 8

THE COLD WAS what finally revived him.

He was lying in a fetal position, twisted on his left side with his knees touching his chest and his right hand between his legs. A tremor racked him. Another. The second straightened his legs in a convulsive movement that sent snow misting up: he was covered with it, a thin white blanket of insulation against the freezing Arctic night.

He couldn't open his eyes; the lids seemed frozen shut. He rolled over and came up onto his knees, throwing off the snow blanket, breaking it up into more misting flakes. Pawed at his eyelids with his mittened left hand and got them unstuck. His vision was blurred; he saw two windlasses, two snow-mantled dumps, two dead fires speckled with white. When he moved his head it seemed to make

a cracking sound, like ice fragmenting. The back of
his neck was numb, but under the numbness he was
aware of a dull ache. He had almost no feeling in
his right hand.

Nausea overtook him. He gagged, vomited up a
thin stream of bile and saliva. Then he got one
snowshoe under him and levered himself up; stood
swaying and trembling, swiping at his eyes again,
trying to bring them into focus. His thoughts were
as blurred and unstable as his vision.

The landscape wavered, then settled into single
images. He realized that the snowfall had quit altogether, that the storm had blown itself out and the
clouds overhead were shifting, breaking up; random stars winked here and there in the black rifts.
The wind had died, too, and the temperature had
climbed ten or fifteen degrees. If that had not happened, if the storm had continued its assault and the
temperature had dropped instead of risen, he would
not be alive now. He would have frozen to death
lying buried there in the snow.

He tried to raise his right arm, couldn't make it
respond. Then he saw that the hand was exposed,
dimly remembered losing his revolver when Thaxter's shot had felled him. Christ! The front of his
parka had been pulled open too, he realized, without understanding how or why.

He closed the parka, then caught hold of the mitten hanging from its string and worked it clumsily

over the numb fingers. Frostbite. But there was no telling yet how bad it was.

How long had he been unconscious? He couldn't tell that either; the moon was still hidden behind the restless clouds. But the remains of the shaft fire weren't even smoldering. Two hours, at least. Thaxter must have thought the rifle bullet had finished him. Either that, or he had decided to leave him there to freeze.

McQuestion's neck had begun to throb: the pain was gathering now as the numbness faded. Gathering also was his rage. His revolver—where was his revolver? He staggered back toward the dead fire. His legs didn't want to work right; the joints felt stiff and atrophied. Each step sent more agony through his head.

He moved back and forth between the windlass and the place where he had lain in the snow, scuffing through the fresh drift, stimulating the sluggish circulation in his legs. But he was still racked with chills. He had to get inside where it was warm, and soon.

It was pure luck that he found his revolver quickly. He caught it up, rubbed it against his parka to rid it of its coating of ice, and holstered it. Then, head bowed, he began to slog toward the shoulder of the hill so he could approach the cabin the way he had left it, through the trees and along the rimrock at its back.

Part of the moon appeared as he skirted the base of the hill. He couldn't see the cabin in its pale, cold shine, but what he did see made him pause in momentary confusion. Sled tracks. Clear in the virgin snowfield, extending away at a sharp angle between the cabin and Two-Willow Creek.

Another visitor, come upcreek from the Chandindu? It didn't seem likely. The tracks must have been made by the sledge belonging to Thaxter and Loomis.

McQuestion came around toward the trees. When he had a clear look at the cabin he saw that its front window was dark. A thin squirrel-tail of smoke came from the stovepipe, evidence of a banked and dying fire within.

It could be that the two men were already bunked up, asleep. McQuestion moved ahead cautiously on his stiff legs, keeping to the heavier shadows. He paused when he neared the animal shelter, but there were no sounds from within. No stirring or barking of dogs either when he passed it by. And the sledge was no longer on the cache on its far side. He went along the back wall of the cabin, turned the corner. The big cache that had been built onto that wall was empty of the mounds of frozen meat he had noticed earlier.

He was sure then that Thaxter and Loomis were gone, but he did not let himself relax until he had kicked open the door and found the interior deserted. His handcuffs lay open on the floor. Thaxter must have taken the handcuff key off him, to release Loomis, while he'd lain unconscious in the snow; that was why his parka had been open. The platform at the rear had been cleared of all the stolen supplies. Most of the two men's personal belongings were also missing; even the bunks had been stripped bare. A dropped and spilled package of black tea testified to the haste with which they had vacated the cabin.

McQuestion lighted the lamp, fed wood into the stove until the sheet iron glowed and heat shimmered through the room. Then he found two pannikins that had been left behind, stepped outside again long enough to fill them with snow, and set both on the stove. He scooped up some of the spilled tea, dropped it into one of the pannikins. Only then did he remove his parka and mittens and take stock of himself, using a jagged piece of mirror that hung on one wall.

Thaxter's bullet had cut a deep furrow along his neck; the furrow was caked with frozen blood and it burned fiercely now. There was a tiny patch of frostbite on one cheek. But despite his fears, his right hand was not frostbitten—just stiffened from the cold. The skin of the fingers was painful to the touch, reddened and slightly swollen, beginning to itch a little; but there was none of the dead-whiteness that meant real frostbite and the likeli-hood of gangrene.

He warmed the hand at the stove, massaging it to stimulate circulation. When the snow melted and the water heated in the one pannikin he immersed the hand in it briefly, until the water became too hot. Then he used the water to swab the frozen blood off his neck, to cleanse the wound.

The tea began to boil in the other pannikin. Mc-Question drank it as hot as he could stand it, to warm himself and to further dilate the blood vessels in his hand and cheek. By the time he finished it the chills that had racked him were gone. His hand tingled and the fingers moved more or less normally. He drew the mitten over it again to keep it warm.

While he made more tea he considered the sudden departure of Thaxter and Loomis. It was plain that they had cleared out with no intention of returning. The reason for that was obvious enough: they hadn't known he had tracked them down on his own, without reporting his findings to division headquarters in Dawson; he hadn't let any of that slip to Loomis earlier. Loomis was a coward—he must have convinced Thaxter that other Redcoats were on the way, that they had no choice except to pack up and run. Not even a man obsessed with the idea of pay dirt to be found on Two-Willow Creek would be willing to stand and fight a whole division of North West Mounted Police.

But where were they headed? If they were afraid the entire Force was after them, there was nowhere in the Yukon for them to hide—even cheechakos had to know that. They would have to try to get out of the Territory, then, and at this time of year there were only two possible routes into Alaska.

The shortest was northwest to Forty-Mile and Fort Cudahy, but there was nothing much on the Alaska side except Circle City and Fort Yukon, both small places, both surrounded by thousands of miles of snow and ice. Little sanctuary for fugitives in that direction.

It seemed much more likely that they would head south up the Yukon River and attempt to leave the Territory via either White Pass into Skagway or the Chilkoot into Dyea. That route meant spending at least another three weeks in the Yukon, but with the small number of Redcoats stationed in the Territory and the travel hardships of winter still prevailing, it was not that great a risk. And once they reached either Skagway or Dyea, they could board a steamship and be Outside in a matter of days, where even the long and persistent arm of the North West Mounted Police would have difficulty reaching them.

Travel hardships, McQuestion thought. And a pair of cheechakos unfamiliar with the rugged, icebound wilderness. No matter which way they headed and even with a good dog team and a sledge loaded down with grub, it would be a grueling, treacherous run. Most veteran Yukoners were loathe to try leaving the Territory during even a mild winter—and this one had been anything but mild.

Would Loomis and Thaxter try it alone? No, it wasn't likely. Thaxter seemed to be a cunning sort, far from stupid. He would have realized that their only chance lay in hiring a seasoned dog-puncher to lead them out. One who asked no questions and was willing to leave on a moment's notice.

There were at least two men in the vicinity of Dawson who fit those requirements. One was Charley Upfield, the man who had identified Loomis's watch fob in the Frontier Saloon yesterday. But Upfield lived in Dawson proper, and it was doubtful Thaxter would want to enter town, believing as he evidently did that the Force had been alerted to him.

The second puncher, Everett Ravenhill, shared a cabin with a prospector named Haldane on Moosehide Creek, some three miles above Dawson. A hard-drinking Englishman who had been in the district several years, Ravenhill had made half a dozen winter trips to Dyea and Skagway, including one for supplies before Christmas; and he had been known to loudly boast in Dawson's saloons that his dog team was the finest in the Territory, that no man could log a faster time between Dawson and Lake Bennett. Even a cheechako such as Thaxter had likely heard of him and would know where to find him . . .

McQuestion drank more tea, then donned his parka and snowshoes again. Thinking about Ravenhill's dog team had reminded him of his own dogs. They should still be where he'd left them, on the other side of the hill facing the cabin; with Thaxter and Loomis thinking he was dead, there wouldn't have been any reason for them to go looking for the team. The malemutes were probably starving by now, but the Siberian was well trained and stronger than any of them: he would have kept them down and waiting at least this long.

Leaving the cabin, McQuestion slogged quickly up to the ridge. He was panting and shivering again by the time he came over the crest. The dogs were where he'd left them, all right, curled in the snow in their traces. Takus stood up first as he caught McQuestion's scent; the others followed suit, shaking off snow, and began to howl for food.

He went down to the sledge. A couple of the dogs had tried to chew through the leather traces, but they hadn't done much damage. McQuestion got onto the runners, found his whip and cracked it; the dogs strained forward, broke the runners from the crust. Took him up over the crown and back down to the cabin.

What he wanted to do after feeding the dogs was to set out immediately on the fugitive's trail. And if he lost it, head upriver to Moosehide Creek and the cabin where Everett Ravenhill lived. If Thaxter and Loomis *had* gone to recruit Ravenhill, it was possible he could catch up with them there.

But he didn't dare go anywhere this night, not if he hoped to survive it. His legs were still wobbly, his head ached, his hand ached, he was trembling from the cold, and he stood on the edge of exhaustion. He needed rest, food, the warmth of the cabin till morning. Out here in the frigid darkness, he was liable to collapse and lose consciousness again. And then he *would* freeze to death.

He unharnessed the dogs, got them into the shelter. Fed and watered them from his own supplies. Forced himself to eat a bannock and some pemmican, washing them down with more hot tea. Put carbolic salve on his neck wound, on his frostbitten cheek, on his hand. Stoked the stove with more cordwood. By the time he was finished with all of this, he was so exhausted he could barely stand. He had dragged his buffalo robe inside; he lay down on one of the bunks and pulled the robe over him.

He was asleep within seconds.

In the morning darkness he awoke stiff and sore

and deviled by half a dozen small pains. But the chills were gone, and he had no fever. Once he was up and moving around, he knew he had regained most of his strength.

Thaxter and Loomis had forgotten a sack of flour in their haste to quit the cabin; McQuestion took it outside and stored it with what was left of his own supplies inside his sledge. He also stored all that they'd left of their dog rations, about thirty pounds of frozen moose meat. Then he got Takus and the malemutes out, snapped them into their traces. And set out along Two-Willow Creek.

Daylight came as he neared the Chandindu River. The bluish-green tint to the snow and the intense black shadows faded into a uniform silver-gray. It had not snowed during the night; the sky, brightened by the pale fan of dawn, was once again clear. Nor had enough of a wind come up to obliterate the tracks left by the runners on the fugitives' sledge. He was able to follow their trail all the way to the confluence of the Chandindu and the Yukon.

There, he found evidence that the two men had turned to the southeast along the Yukon, toward Dawson. He raced along the river ice, riding the sledge more than usual to conserve his strength, traveling in a kind of ghostly silence except for the thin whine of the runners. The edge of the sun was up when he reached Moosehide Creek. The cabin

Ravenhill shared with Jim Haldane was less than a mile above the mouth, sheltered by trees and fronted by salmonberry shrubs. Haldane's diggings, marked by windlass and dump and blazing fire, were nearby. McQuestion found him there, scooping snow into a cut-down tin propped at the fire's edge.

Haldane was a bear of a man wearing a slitted wooden eye shield as protection against snow glare. His mouth turned crooked when McQuestion asked him about Thaxter and Loomis. "Sure, them two cheechakos was here," he said. "Showed up past midnight, woke Ev and me out of a sound sleep. I damn near shot 'em both for trespassing."

"Looking for Ravenhill?"

"Yup. Told Ev they was near broke, their claim was skunk, and they couldn't see no point in sticking it out until summer." Haldane spat into the fire. "Crazy cheechakos," he said. "And Ev just as crazy to agree to guide 'em. But you know how Ev is. Good sense ain't something he was born with."

McQuestion nodded. "They say where they wanted to go?"

"Alaska, is all," Haldane said. "Skagway or Dyea, I reckon."

"What time did they leave?"

"Couple of hours after they got here. They was in a big hurry. Struck me as kind of peculiar, but Ev didn't seem to mind. Once he's stirred up to something, he don't like delays."

"What about grub for the dogs? Did Ravenhill have enough here or was he planning to pick some up elsewhere?"

"He loaded about three hundred pounds of frozen fish," Haldane said. "All we could spare; I'll be needing the rest for my own team. He was fixing to stop at Blind John's claim over on Hunker. You know Blind John?"

"Yes."

"Well, John's got a cache of frozen horsemeat. Been using it to trade for grub. Ev figured to swap him flour and fat bacon for the rest of what he'll need for his outfit and the cheechakos'."

McQuestion thanked him and got back onto the sledge.

Haldane said, "Say, you after them two fellas, Corporal?"

"I am."

"What for, you don't mind my asking? Ev ain't mixed himself up with a couple of hardcases, has he?"

"Ravenhill can take care of himself," McQuestion said evasively, and cracked his whip to start the dogs before Haldane could ask any more questions.

Back on the Yukon, he mushed the team hard through the bright, cold morning, past Dawson, and upriver along the Klondike. When he reached Blind

John's claim on Hunker Creek he found the one-eyed sourdough taking breakfast in his cabin. Ravenhill and his two charges had been there toward dawn, and had made the swap of grub for dog rations. Blind John still had plenty of the frozen horsemeat left in his cache; McQuestion appropriated four hundred pounds, signing a paper that would allow the prospector reimbursement in cash or trade goods at the police barracks in Dawson. He also appropriated a hundred pounds of grub for himself, most of it flour and beans. Blind John was none too pleased with the arrangement, but he did more grumbling than arguing. The last thing he or any sourdough wanted was trouble with the Redcoats.

An hour later, McQuestion neared Dawson again. He thought briefly of veering over there, reporting to Colonel Steele as regulations dictated. But that would waste precious time; Thaxter and Loomis already had a half day's lead on him, and with Everett Ravenhill leading them, it would be damned difficult as it was to catch them before they reached Alaskan soil. There was also the possibility that Steele would be angry enough to restrict him to quarters. McQuestion might have risked that if telegraph lines had been strung between Dawson and the other Mounted Police outposts—particularly the ones at the summits of White Pass and the Chilkoot—but such a communications link was still in the planning stages, a year or two away. There was no way Steele could notify the Redcoats between Dawson and the Alaska border that two fugitives were headed their way. So it was up to McQuestion, just as he had felt it to be all along.

He bypassed Dawson and plunged on without slowing.

CHAPTER 9

IT TOOK MCQUESTION a little better than three weeks to make the three-hundred-and-eighty-mile trek to Lake Bennett, where the Skagway trail veered off to White Pass. Three long, frustrating weeks, because he neither caught up with the trio he was pursuing nor saw any sign of them other than the remains of their camps.

Between Dawson and Fort Selkirk he set a hard pace, twelve hours at a stretch, traveling by darkness as well as by daylight, logging an average of forty miles between stops. He drove the dogs hard; fed them only at night because well-fed dogs were lazy. At each camp he had to tend to their bruised feet, wipe out little balls of ice that had gathered between their toes. But he drove himself just as hard, so that at the end of the day he was leg-weary, his arms stiff and sore from working the heavy sledge. He kept his sore hand mittened as much as possible, and after the first couple of days he had no trouble with it. The bullet furrow on his neck was healing, too; he kept it covered and treated with carbolic salve to prevent infection.

The two hundred miles between Selkirk and Lake Laberge proved much more difficult. The Yukon swept downward from one shelving plateau to another and successive ice terraces had built up, with a number of jams and stretches of open water. One of the jams was massive—a series of ice hills that extended for two or three miles; McQuestion had to constantly veer the sledge away from up-ended ice cakes, and in places he was forced to hoist it bodily over hummocks. The temperature held at better than twenty below and the cold made the portage all the more arduous. So did heavy fog that hung over the open stretches of water. He spent the better part of a day covering no more than five miles.

Four days out of Selkirk the ice jams grew more frequent, more troublesome to cross. Above each was a section of fast-moving water; heavy rim ice had formed beside these sections. Sometimes he was able to traverse the ice, but where the current swept in against the sheer banks he had to break trail away from the river. Traveling inland was slower than across rough ice: the snow was so cottony in places that McQuestion had to mush several times along a section of trail before it was solid enough to hold the dogs and the sledge.

On the fifty-mile stretch below Lake Laberge, dangerous ice bridges that had formed above swift water restricted McQuestion's travel to the daylight hours. He managed to traverse them without incident. The only mishap he suffered was a twisted ankle on the eighteenth day, when he broke a snowshoe harness on an ice hummock. It was a minor sprain—and he had an extra pair of snowshoes on the sledge—but the accident cost him yet another few hours he felt he could ill afford.

Until he reached Lake Laberge, the only other human beings he saw were a few scattered sourdoughs, a pair of traders near Fort Selkirk, and a group of stranded gold hunters at the head of Thirty-Mile Rapids. He found an encampment of several hundred men at Lake Laberge, men who had moved up from Lake Bennett and Lake Lindeman in the hopes of stealing a march on the main body of stampeders. McQuestion considered stopping at the Lake Laberge police post, to leave a message for Colonel Steele and to ask the sergeant in charge if he had seen Ravenhill and his party come through; but he decided against it. It would only waste more time. Ravenhill knew the river better than he did, but the inexperience of Thaxter and Loomis would have slowed them up to some extent.

They could be as much as a day and a half ahead of him by now, or they could be no more than a few hours. He would wait to find out until he got to Lake Bennett—and he would wait to leave a message until he reached the summit outpost on either White Pass or the Chilkoot.

He arrived at Lake Tagish, just above Bennett, late on the twenty-first day and weariness forced him to make camp for the night there. He was almost out of rations by this time; some flour and salt and less than fifty pounds of dog food was all he had left. Before dawn the next morning he mushed on to Lake Bennett. And what he saw when he reached it was an awesome sight.

Thousands of tents of every size and type—army tents, dog tents, bell tents, pup tents, canvas lean-tos, even what appeared to be a circus marquee—encircled the lake. A tent city that housed not only thousands of stampeders but a variety of merchants and entrepreneurs: he saw saloon tents, gambling tents, barber tents, hotel tents, café tents. A sea of white and gray and brown, enclosed by barren, crenelated mountain peaks, whipped by savage winds that swept down from the higher ice fields.

Piled between the tents were crates of food and tinned goods, furniture, sheet-iron and Yukon stoves, mining equipment, miscellaneous personal belongings in snow-covered mounds. And oxen, pigs, goats, chickens, mules, horses. And piles,

stacks, wigwams of logs and cut lumber, like a vast
and haphazard lumberyard. Everywhere McQuestion looked along the shore he saw boats and rafts
being built, some finished, some still skeletal. Men
swarmed over the surrounding hills, laboriously
felling frozen trees. Dozens of platform sawpits had
been erected, on which other men used whipsaws to
produce rough-dressed planks; there was even a
small sawmill built back on one of the hillsides.
The thunder of falling timber, the rasp and pound of
tools, the shouts of men and the cries of animals
created a constant pulse of sound.

McQuestion mushed his weary dogs across the
slushy surface of the lake, dodging sail-equipped
ice sleds. There was no police post here; he would
have to make a random canvass of the stampeders
to determine where Ravenhill and his two charges
had gone.

The Skagway trail was closest—you had to
make difficult portage through a boulder-strewn
canyon to get to Lake Lindeman and the Dyea
trail—and so he went first to that end of the lake.
Hundreds of gold seekers worked there, many of
them wearing slitted wooden masks to protect their
eyes from snow glare, others with charcoal smeared
over their whiskered faces to prevent sunburn. They
struck McQuestion as strange, otherworldly beings.
And in a way, they *were* from a world alien to
him—a world where the promise of glittering yel-

low metal uprooted men and sent them rushing thousands of miles from home, into months of hardship in an icebound wilderness. Gold fever. It was a malady McQuestion had never been afflicted with and would never quite understand.

He stopped at several of the sawpits, spoke to the men wielding the big, heavy whipsaws. None of them had seen Ravenhill and his party. Nor had any of the two-score other stampeders he talked to during the next hour.

Frustration and impatience were sharp in him by the time he approached a pair of young men who were caulking a finished boat with oakum. Brothers, from the look of them—both towheaded, muscular, their faces so blackened with charcoal that they resembled minstrel show performers. At first, when McQuestion identified himself, they were wary and taciturn, as many of the others had been; but when he asked them about the three men, curiosity and a natural loquaciousness loosened them up. And they gave him the answers he was looking for.

"I saw 'em, all right," the taller of the two said. "You remember, Hank? Three men, two sleds in tandem."

The one named Hank nodded. "I'm not likely to forget a handlebar mustache like that one fellow had. Biggest damn thing I ever laid eyes on."

That was Ravenhill, all right.

McQuestion asked, "When did you see them?"

"Yesterday afternoon. Just before dark."

"Where were they headed?"

"Toward the trail to White Pass," the tall one said. "Wouldn't you say, Hank?"

"I would," Hank said. "Headed straight for the pass."

McQuestion cursed silently. Now that he knew their destination, it did him no good. They had a lead of better than twelve hours; he hadn't picked up any time on them at all. Damn Ravenhill and his trail savvy! They were well into Alaska by now— and they would likely be well out of it on board a steamer by the time he reached Skagway.

He spurned questions from the two brothers, left them, and drove his dogs toward the Skagway trail. It was forty-five miles across White Pass to the coast, but they were miles as rugged as any he'd traveled so far: tortuous switchbacks that skirted cliffsides, plunged through bogs and among huge boulders and shale outcroppings, crossed and re-crossed bodies of water, traversed canyon and valley, summit and slope, with dozens of obstacles along the way. And judging from the straggling line of men and animals coming down out of the pass above, most of the trail would be jammed. Even if the weather remained clear and dry, he couldn't hope to reach Skagway before the day after tomorrow.

He mushed up through the first pass, down into the Tutshi Valley and across it. A thousand-foot climb up Turtle Mountain, then down again along a narrow trail that wound around a network of tiny lakes. Then he could see Summit Hill—another thousand-foot climb, this one barred by great slabs of granite and a welter of sharp-edged rocks.

The scale to the summit took more than an hour. The Mounted Police post, a single log cabin with a wind-lashed Union Jack flying from its roof, marked the end of Canadian soil. Two other cabins had been built into the mountainside to house the Redcoats on duty up here. One of them manned a Maxim gun on a tabletop ledge above the post, as a safeguard against any trouble that might develop at the border.

McQuestion didn't recognize the man on the Maxim; he moved his team ahead to the post building. He did recognize two of the three men at the border station, one of whom was the sergeant in charge, Stanley Threadgold. A long line of men and animals, outlined blackly against the whiteness of the snow, their breaths making clouds of vapor in the icy air, extended down the Alaska side of the trail and out of sight. Cheechakos, each bearing enough supplies to last six months—a ton of goods per man, as decreed by Colonel Steele to prevent starvation and just the kind of murder-for-grub that Thaxter and Loomis had perpetrated. Professional mule packers and porters, most of them Chilkat Indians who charged a dollar a pound to bring goods across the passes from Skagway and Dyea. Traders carrying clothing, pots and pans, coal oil, candles, hundreds of other necessities, and a variety of luxury items. Tinkers, barbers, lawyers, gamblers, restaurateurs, bartenders, perhaps a doctor or two. And thieves, sure-thing men—parasites who had been bred in the swampy backwaters of San Francisco and Seattle, and in Soapy Smith's Skagway. All lured and sustained by the cry of gold, the promise of easy riches.

The Redcoats checked each man through, methodically, to make sure he had brought the requisite provisions. They examined horses and pack animals, for regulations demanded that sore or injured animals be immediately shot if brought across the border into Canada. They also conducted spot checks for illegal whiskey: some traders tried to smuggle it in in quantity.

It was arduous duty, manning a summit outpost, and even though this one had been open only a short while, McQuestion saw the strain reflected in Threadgold's somber young face. Threadgold had been recruited from among the adventurous and ne'er-do-well offspring of British aristocracy, and he had been used to more genteel surroundings at home and again on the Force in Ottawa, before being transferred to the Yukon the previous year.

He was a good officer—and a smart one, or he would not have made the rank of sergeant as quickly as he had—but he still had not quite adapted to life on the wilderness frontier.

He seemed pleased to see McQuestion, not in any personal sense but because it allowed him to spend a few minutes inside the post, in front of a hot stove and away from the packed and grumbling mass of humanity outside. He provided tea and a bowl of stew; then, while McQuestion ate, he stood warming himself and staring out through the rimed window at the border station.

"Wretches," he said, "poor addled fools. How many of them can hope to make their fortune, really?"

"Not many," McQuestion said around a mouthful of stew. "Hardly any of them."

"Yes. But none of those chaps will believe it. They refuse to understand the futility of what they're about."

"Some of them understand it too well."

"The grafters, you mean? Yes, you're right. But we can't keep them out either, can we. Nor stop them from committing their bloody crimes."

"We can stop some of them, Sergeant."

"But only after the fact," Threadgold said.

"Maybe so. But the more of them we arrest, the fewer people they can harm. We have to see to it that they forfeit their freedom no matter what the cost."

"If you mean the cost in lives, that's a bit extreme, isn't it?"

"I mean the personal cost," McQuestion said. "The cost to us in time and strain and hardship."

"Well," Threadgold said after a few seconds. "You seem a bit on edge. Would it be a manhunt that brings you here from Dawson, Corporal?"

"Yes. Two men, William Thaxter and Floyd Loomis. I have reason to believe they came over the pass sometime last night, headed for Skagway."

"What have they done?"

"Murder," McQuestion said, and let it go at that. "You know Everett Ravenhill, don't you, Sergeant? Well, he was guiding them."

"Ravenhill? Yes, I know him. He came through last night, just as you say, with a party of two men."

"At what time?"

"Quite late. Midnight, I should say. There was a squabble at a campsite downtrail and I had to go out and settle it. Ravenhill and his party came by as I was returning."

"Did you speak with him?"

"We exchanged pleasantries," Threadgold said. "The other two chaps had nothing to say. Out of their hearing, I asked Ravenhill why he should risk traveling at night; he said the two men were cheechakos who had had enough of prospecting and couldn't wait to leave the north country. He seemed to treat the whole business as a joke. I can't believe a chap like Ravenhill is involved in murder . . ."

"I'm sure he isn't, Sergeant. And I doubt he knows the truth about Thaxter and Loomis."

"I see."

Threadgold seemed on the verge of asking particulars. Before he could, McQuestion invoked Colonel Steele's name, saying that he wanted to leave a message for Steele to be transported to Dawson with a Redcoat or the next trustworthy dog-puncher who came through. The implication was that he was on a mission at Steele's orders, and Threadgold took it that way. If McQuestion had told him the truth, the sergeant might have tried to keep him from leaving Canada, pending word from division headquarters. Like Steele, Threadgold treated the police manual as a religious man treated his Bible: he lived by the Word.

McQuestion wrote out his message, keeping it brief. He explained what he had learned about Thaxter and Loomis, what had happened at Two-Willow Creek, and what his own intentions were; that was all. Then he signed it, sealed the message into an envelope, wrote Steele's name on the outside, and handed the envelope to the sergeant.

Threadgold said, "You're welcome to spend the night here, Corporal. The barracks aren't much, really, but they are more comfortable than camping on the trail."

"Thank you, but I'd rather push on."

"You don't intend to try crossing Devil's Hill until morning, do you? The trail there is dangerous enough by daylight; at night it would be suicidal."

"Would Ravenhill try to cross it after dark?"

"Certainly not."

"Then I won't either, Sergeant."

Outside again, McQuestion mushed his dogs ahead into Alaska, past the long line of stampeders waiting at a standstill, faces grim and weary, like a company of ravaged foot soldiers on their way into one more battle.

A short while later, as he passed an encampment at the base of Summit Hill and began the ascent up Porcupine Hill, the roiling clouds opened up and a light rain started to fall.

CHAPTER 10

THE COASTAL WINDS made it warmer on this side of the mountains. The trail across Porcupine Hill was unfrozen, muddy, churned up by the constant plodding steps of thousands of men and animals. Snow still clung to the high rocks, still filled the canyons and bogs, still lay in patches and pockets elsewhere. But if the rain and the warm temperatures continued, most of it below the summit would be gone in another couple of weeks.

Something else littered the terrain, too: a grisly spectacle of animal carcasses. Horses, mules, oxen, goats, even a few reindeer with their horns amputated that had been sold to gullible cheechakos in Skagway as mules—all lying stiff and bloody and bloated among boulders and defiles, in the canyons below. The area resembled a battlefield after heavy skirmishing and cannon fire. Some of the animals had died of exhaustion; the stampeders treated them with savage cruelty, allowing them to stand hungry and fully loaded for days at a stretch, beating them when they wouldn't obey. Others had made missteps and plunged to their deaths or had broken legs and either been brained with rocks or left to die in slow agony. It would be worse later in the spring and during the summer, McQuestion thought, when the main army of gold seekers came swarming over the pass.

The senseless carnage enraged and sickened him. He was a man who cared for animals, understood them, mostly preferred them to the company of men. Animals, at least, did not kill with wanton brutality in the pursuit of pieces of yellow metal.

It was full dark by the time he reached the westward foot of Porcupine Hill. The light, steady rain thickened the blackness, gave it a gumbolike quality; visibility was no more than a few yards, except where the trail was weirdly lighted by fires the stampeders had built in sheltered cutbanks and narrow draws nearby.

The men watched him sullenly as he passed, huddled in close to their fires for warmth, their faces shadowed inside hooded mackinaws. None spoke to him. Now and then he heard curses, raised voices bickering over supplies or wood gathering.

Once he saw a man using a heavy willow stick to

beat an exhausted, pack-laden horse, so as to move it out of his way, and he stopped and told the man to desist. The gold hunter cursed him, saying, "You got no authority here, Redcoat, you can't tell me what to do." McQuestion wrenched the stick out of his hands, hurled it away into the night; stood looking at the man without further words. It was no contest: the stampeder turned away, muttering to himself, and hid behind his fire.

McQuestion found a place to make camp, under a fan-shaped overhang. Built his fire and pitched his fly. He brewed tea but fixed nothing to eat; Threadgold's stew had quelled his appetite. He lay huddled under his buffalo robe, watching the misty rain spill down beyond the fire, listening to small, occasional rumblings somewhere in the mountains that told of snowslides. He would have liked to smoke his pipe, but he had long ago used up the last of his tobacco.

Sleep was some time away—and when it finally did come it was crowded with images of Molly, Thaxter, Loomis. And Eileen. And the tall man with the lightning-fork scar on his neck, whose name may or may not have been George Blanton and who did not have a face.

The rain stopped during the night and the dawn was cold and misty. As McQuestion packed his sledge and then set out for Devil's Hill, there were more distant rumblings. They made him edgy. None of the slides seemed to be nearby, but they could happen anywhere up here, at any time.

More animal carcasses flanked the trail to Devil's Hill. Here and there in the canyons, flocks of crows picked at what was left of the flesh, screeching and fighting with one another. Dead Horse Trail, McQuestion thought. That was what it ought to be called, as a bitter reminder of what happened when men lusted after gold.

He reached Devil's Hill and started up the trail that wound along the sides of sheer slate cliffs, letting the dogs move at their own careful pace. Threadgold had been right about not attempting to travel it at night. Already it was narrowing to a few feet in width; there was barely enough room for men and animals to pass safely, and it was littered with obstacles.

The ascent was steep, with the trail corkscrewing its way around the cliffs. The wind blew in gusts, driving wet mist across a crepe-gray sky. In places the drop-offs were dizzying, hundreds of feet into the boulder-filled canyons. The stampeders had fallen into line again on their slow march to the Yukon; twice on the slender trail McQuestion had to stop and hold the dogs still while heavily laden packhorses were led past.

Near the trail's crest he passed beneath a cornice of snow well up on the heights. It had a bloated, unstable look that scraped at his nerves until he was clear of its shadow. Some distance ahead the path widened briefly before it began its switchbacking descent, and where boulders protected the open side he stopped to rest the dogs and flex some of the tautness out of his arms and back. He was sweating inside his clothing from the exertion of the climb.

As he stood stretching, another low-pitched rumbling began. Grew louder, more ominous. The muscles bunched again across his shoulders. Close, this one. Above, behind him, and very close: that swollen cornice . . .

Somebody out of his sight downtrail began yelling frantically, "Snowslide, snowslide!"

The men near McQuestion had quit moving and were exchanging fearful looks, tilting their heads to stare up into the misty wastes above. He shouted at them to stay where they were, gave the dogs a sharp-voiced command to lie down, and ran back along the path. The booming was louder now, like rolling thunderclaps. More men were yelling; three of them came diving back around the switchback just ahead, knocking over others in the line. Mc-Question fought past them, turned the corner to where he could see the cornice again.

It was moving. A widening section of bare rock, like a massive scar, had appeared above it as the snow settled and began to slide. The mass seemed to revolve; the noise was a full-throated roar now, full of hissings and scrapings as the avalanche gained momentum.

More stampeders came rushing and stumbling back this way, half wild with terror, their pack animals abandoned below. Others had turned the opposite way, were struggling downtrail into the men ahead of them; one piled into an overburdened mule, sent it braying over the edge and almost went over himself. But a few of the damn fools, in confusion or panic or cowardice, had pressed themselves into niches in the cliff face directly beneath the oncoming juggernaut. McQuestion yelled at them to get the hell away, but the rush and roar of the slide swallowed his words so that he did not even hear them himself, only felt them raw and futile in his throat.

The revolving mass picked up trees and boulders, consumed them or hurled them into the air as if they were matchsticks and pebbles. Its onrushing speed was awesome. It was too late for McQuestion to do anything except turn and run himself. He scrambled over writhing bodies, managed to get up around the switchback and out of harm's way just as the avalanche came sweeping past with a deafening, earthshaking roar.

The trail disappeared in a churning sea of white. Snow clouds choked the air like dense white smoke. Moments later the thunder faded, finally ceased altogether—and the stillness that remained was breathless, electrically charged, almost as terrifying as the slide itself because it was the stillness of death.

McQuestion made sure his dogs were all right, then groped his way back downtrail, around the turning in the cliff wall. But he couldn't see anything; the air was still clogged with a fog of snow particles that blotted out the mountainside, blotted out everything more than a few feet away. He kept moving forward, feeling his way along the sheer rock. It was as if he were moving through something semisolid; he could feel the snow particles stinging like wood slivers in his lungs.

He had gone fewer than fifty feet when he came up against the barrier. He thought of the men who had been huddled there against the cliffside—dead men now, crushed under tons of snow and rock. There was nothing that could be done for any of them. But it was possible others caught by the avalanche had survived. Men at its periphery, who hadn't quite made it out of the way of the onslaught.

The air had started to clear, the flinty particles settling around him. He could hear the shouts and cries of men, both behind him and, as if from a great distance, from beyond the barrier. A thin, bearded man came up alongside him, his face pale with shock. Others were there, too, moving sluggishly, not speaking, staring at the massive fan of snow and rock with the awe of men witnessing nature's might for the first time. On the barrier's far side, through the shimmering crystals, McQuestion could see the shapes of other stampeders standing in a similar pose.

"You men!" he yelled across at them. "This is Corporal McQuestion, North West Mounted Police! Organize yourselves over there! Get shovels out of your packs, start hunting for survivors!"

Shuffling movement. Then someone called back an affirmative.

McQuestion turned to the gold seekers near him. "The same goes for you men. Step lively now. We've no time to waste."

They obeyed; they were too benumbed by the avalanche and their own narrow escape to offer any arguments. The subsequent search uncovered one survivor, half buried, with a broken leg—and two corpses. McQuestion judged that there were at least four or five more dead under the snow and rock or down in the canyon below.

The stampeders on the uphill side where Mc-Question was either had to keep on digging into the barrier, in order to clear the trail so they could continue, or return en masse to Skagway. They chose to stay and dig, as McQuestion had known they would. He left orders with them to transport the bodies they had found, and any others that were uncovered, to the summit for proper burial. Perhaps the instructions would be carried out and perhaps they wouldn't; the pursuit of gold was all that really mattered to these men. But he could not afford to stay and see that it was done himself.

By the time he set out down the opposite face of Devil's Hill, toward the wagon road that would take him over flat timberland and swampland into Skagway, hours had passed since the avalanche and it was growing dark again. More time lost. More time for Thaxter and Loomis to have made good their escape from Skagway.

CHAPTER 11

SKAGWAY WAS NOT at all as McQuestion remembered it. The setting was the same: it had been built on a wooded flat where the Skagway River emptied into the placid waters of Skagway Bay. Ships were still anchored on the bay, and men still swarmed over the beach, freighting supplies from one point to another. But everything else had changed.

When he'd come here ten months ago, to bring a trader back to Dawson to stand trial for shooting a Siwash, Skagway had been a confusion of hovels and tents, with a single muddy street along which were four makeshift saloons, a blacksmith's shop, a doctor's tent, a restaurant with its menu hand-painted on the seat of a pair of ragged man's trousers, a few campsites, plenty of tree stumps, and an impermanent population mostly composed of stampeders. Now there were a network of streets, rows of frame buildings, upward of a hundred saloons, a newspaper, and, at the last Mounted Police estimate, more than five thousand residents. A mile-long wharf had been built out over the tidal flats, so that most of the constant stream of incoming boats would have a place to dock and passengers and animals wouldn't be forced to swim ashore, as had been the case last year. It was a full-fledged town.

But not a good town. One of the meanest, most lawless settlements anywhere—a "hell on earth," as Colonel Steele had once called it, where murders, muggings, swindlings, and blatant thievery were commonplace. The domain of Soapy Smith and his band of cutthroats.

The Mounted Police had a thick file on Smith, in the event he sought to extend his operations into the Yukon—not an unlikely possibility, given the man's audacity. He was a former Texas cowhand who had first turned shellgame grafter, then moved into the Colorado goldfields in the 1880s and branched out into other confidence games, one of which involved selling small cubes of soap for a dollar each on the bogus claim that ten percent of them contained twenty-dollar bills. He had made a fortune robbing Leadville miners; and the soap swindle had given him his nickname.

In the late 1880s he had moved to Denver,

opened a gambling hall, and along with a few lieutenants—"Judge" Norman Van Horn, Doc Baggs,
the "Reverend" Charles Bowers—formed the city's
roughest criminal gang. When the Colorado mining
camp of Creede began to boom in 1892, Smith
moved his operations there. And when word of the
Yukon strike reached them early last year, the gang
had descended on Skagway, literally taken over the
town, and begun fleecing sourdoughs and
cheechakos alike, using any number of bunco
ploys, crooked games of chance, and outright assault and murder.

Smith and his men got away with it because
there was no law in this part of Alaska other than a
single United States marshal and his deputy. He
wouldn't have got away with it in the Yukon; the
Redcoats would long since have broken up his or-
ganization and seen Smith and his lieutenants hung.
Steele and *his* lieutenants maintained their hope
that Smith would be foolhardy enough to try moving into the Yukon one of these days. He would be
made short shrift of if he did. If he stayed put in
Skagway, a declaration of martial law was what it
would take to end his little empire—either that or
an organized vigilante group.

It was the morning after the avalanche when
McQuestion mushed into the dominion of Soapy
Smith. It was spring here: the temperature was well
above zero, most of the ground snow had melted,

and bright green grass was everywhere. The muddy main street, Broadway, was jammed with men, horses, freight wagons. He bypassed it, went down to the docks to mingle with the ant swarm there.

What he learned, even though it was what he'd expected, turned his mood darker than it already was. Three ships had left for Seattle during the past twenty-four hours; Thaxter and Loomis could have had their pick. And no one remembered seeing men who answered to their description.

McQuestion drove the dogs back up to Broadway and went looking for Ravenhill. It was the Englishman's custom to do some celebrating after one of his runs between Dawson and the Alaska coast— that was common knowledge. And celebrating to Ravenhill meant whiskey and faro, massive indulgences in each over at least a forty-eight hour span. As early as it was, he should be in one of Skagway's saloons right now. Whether or not he was sober enough to hold a conversation remained to be seen.

Before he began his search, McQuestion automatically eliminated any of Soapy Smith's drinking and gambling parlors. Ravenhill knew better than to try to buck faro games so openly crooked or to imbibe whiskey so patently cheap. But that still left him with close to a hundred other establishments spread out across the town.

There was no sign of Ravenhill in the first two dozen places he tried, although the bartender in the Northern Star claimed to have seen him late last night. McQuestion kept moving down Broadway, past the Bureau of Information, the Telegraph Office, the Merchants Exchange, the Reliable Packers—all bogus operations set up by Soapy Smith to bilk incoming stampeders. Past a pawnbroker's shop, too, jammed with goods turned in by disillusioned or fleeced cheechakos, its sign proclaiming in fat letters:

KEELAR THE MONEY KING HAS
BARRELS OF MONEY
BUYS AND SELLS EVERYTHING
LOANS MONEY, SELLS BY AUCTION
IS A PUBLIC BENEFACTOR

Sometime past noon he entered Clancey's Northlights Saloon and Dance Hall. The place was crowded, thickly hazed with tobacco smoke, noisy with upraised voices, the tinny beat of a pianola, the whirr of roulette wheels and the rattle of dice, and the off-key singing of "And Her Golden Hair Was Hanging Down Her Back" by half a dozen blowsy slammerkins in imitation Paris Follies dresses. This was where he finally found Ravenhill: holding court at a side-wall table, telling ribald stories to an appreciative audience of cheechakos and rouged and powdered hostesses.

Ravenhill was drunk; that was plain by the look of his eyes, the droop of his magnificent foot-long mustache, the faint slur of his words. But he was still sober enough to immediately recognize McQuestion. He lumbered to his feet, a huge man well above six feet and two hundred pounds, with long hair the same tawny color as his mustache. He poked out one of his hands and grinned lopsidedly.

"The goddamned Redcoats have arrived," he said in his tolerable bellow. "Zack McQuestion, the pride of the bleedin' North West Mounted Police, *if* you please."

The cheechakos and hostesses laughed. Ignoring them, McQuestion shook the offered hand. He liked Ravenhill; the man was irreverent, undisciplined, full of bluster and nonsense much of the time, but he was a decent sort for all of that. A man who could be honest with you if you were honest with him. A man who could be trusted.

"Can we talk alone, Ev?"

"Alone? Hell, lad, it's a party you've walked in on here. In honor of Dame Fortune and the fine chap, whoever he may be, who invented faro."

"How much did you win?"

"Five hundred, thereabouts. Sit down, McQuestion, have a drink on the house's money. We'll toast the ruddy Queen and all her ruddy ancestors."

"I need to talk to you alone," McQuestion said. "It's important."

"It is, is it? What's it about?"

"The two men you brought in from Dawson."

Ravenhill frowned. "What about 'em?"

"They're wanted. That's why I'm here, Ev. I was on your trail all the way, less than a day behind."

"The ruddy hell you were," Ravenhill said, surprised. He shooed off his drunken audience, promising them more liquor and stories later on. When he and McQuestion were alone and seated across from each other he said, "Now then, what've those cheechakos done?"

"Murder," McQuestion said. "You heard about Molly Malone? Well, Thaxter and Loomis are the ones who shot her and her Siwash helpers."

It took a few seconds for Ravenhill to absorb the words. He stared at McQuestion. Then some of the liquor glaze cleared from his eyes, and he rubbed his mouth out of shape and said softly, "Damn my soul! I had no idea, McQuestion, I swear it. Not an inkling."

"I believe you."

"The buggers said they'd given up on a skunk claim on Indian River and wanted clear of the Yukon before the last of their dust and grub ran out and stranded 'em. I took 'em at their lying word."

"You had no reason not to," McQuestion said. "Don't blame yourself."

"A ruddy fool, that's what I am. All that grub they were carrying . . . it came from Molly's road-house?"

"Yes."

"Well, I thought it was odd they'd have that much. After the winter we've been through, a pair of cheechakos oughtn't to've had a quarter of that left over."

"What did you take them for? Hoarders?"

"Right," Ravenhill said unhappily. "Evil of me to deal with that sort too, eh? But it'd been a rum go for me since Christmas. Boredom, you know; I needed a bit of a challenge. I'll confess I didn't do much considering before I took 'em up on their offer."

"Which was what?"

"Fifty dollars in dust—all they had, they said— and whatever they could get here from the sale of their outfit and what was left of the grub. Came to another hundred, after they bought passage Out-side. They should've got more for their dogs, even at Skagway prices, but they were in too much of a rush to haggle."

"They're both long gone by now, I suppose?"

"They are," Ravenhill said with a mixture of anger and remorse. He looked at one of the bottles of whiskey that was sitting on the table, but he made no move toward it. "And good riddance, too, I thought. Goddamn it, I thought they'd changed my ruddy luck!"

"When did they leave?" McQuestion asked.

"Yesterday noon."

"On the same ship?"

Ravenhill nodded. "*Pride of Seattle*, it was called. Scabrous old bucket."

"Bound for Seattle, then?"

"Yes."

"Did either of them let slip where they were headed after they got there?"

"No. I didn't wish the buggers bon voyage."

"They give you trouble, did they?"

"Some at first," Ravenhill said. "The big one, Thaxter, was used to having his way. But not on the trail; I made that clear to him, and he bloody well backed down."

"Did they talk much?"

"Not to me. Closemouthed pair." Ravenhill paused, scowling, as if something had begun to stir in his memory. "Wait a bit. I did overhear the little one, Loomis, say something about a rooming house . . ."

"Where? In Seattle?"

"Yes. Run by a woman he knows—relative of some sort, I gathered. He was telling Thaxter about her one night below Thirty-Mile Rapids."

"Can you remember the woman's name?"

"Tillie something. Name of a country . . . Right: Holland. Tillie Holland."

"Did he mention an address?"

"Not that I heard."

"Or anything else about Tillie Holland?"

Ravenhill shook his head. He was sober now, and his big, flat face was troubled and forlorn. He glanced again at the whiskey bottle, gave his head another shake, stroked his mustache, finally took papers and tobacco from his shirt pocket. McQuestion watched him roll a cigarette with fingers that were not quite steady.

"Goddamn them to hell," Ravenhill said. "I liked Molly. She was a fine lady."

"Yes. She was."

Neither of them spoke for a few seconds. Ravenhill struck a lucifer, fired his cigarette, and sat staring at the burning tip. The pianola continued its tinny beat; the slammerkins were singing a bawdy French song now.

At length Ravenhill said, "You'll be going after 'em, of course?"

"Yes. On the next available steamer. But I'll need a couple of favors first. Can I count on you?"

"You ruddy well can. What can I do?"

"Loan me three hundred dollars from your winnings. I'll have to have that much for passage, civilian clothing, and expenses when I reach Seattle. And I've only a few Canadian dollars with me."

"Done," Ravenhill said.

"There's also my outfit. I could leave it with the United States marshal here, but I don't know how long I'll be gone. It would be better if you'd take the dogs back into the Yukon for me. Turn them over at one of the summit outposts, or use them to haul freight all the way to Dawson if you like."

"Leave that to me." Ravenhill reached over and tapped the whiskey bottle with a blunt forefinger. "And you needn't worry about this. I'll stay sober until I've got back to Dawson."

"I wasn't worried," McQuestion said.

They stood, made their way through the crowded saloon and out into the gray afternoon. Across the way, on Sixth Street just off Broadway, there was a good deal of activity in and around a place called Jeff's Oyster Parlor. McQuestion knew the restaurant by reputation; and as they cut down that way, he recognized the man with the black beard smoking a seegar in front. A tall, slender man, dressed in somber black, with a diamond stickpin in his cravat and a heavy gold watch chain across his vest. The scourge of Skagway himself, Soapy Smith.

McQuestion stared hard at the man as he and Ravenhill passed. One of these days the law would be after Smith, just as McQuestion was after Thaxter and Loomis. And the law would get him, just as he would get Molly's murderers—sooner or later, one way or another. Then Skagway could grow into a decent town.

Smith didn't return McQuestion's stare, didn't even know McQuestion existed. Well, neither did Thaxter and Loomis now, after having left him for dead on Two-Willow Creek. It was the way he wanted it. A hunter's task was always easier when his prey had no idea they were being stalked.

With the three hundred dollars Ravenhill gave him, McQuestion outfitted himself for travel, took a room in the same boardinghouse where Ravenhill was staying, and put his dogs up with the Englishman's. At the wharf again, he learned that there were no Seattle-bound ships leaving until morning. But he did find the captain of one scheduled to depart at dawn, an old salt named Murray, and booked passage with him.

Ravenhill insisted on buying dinner. He was still upset over his unwitting part in the escape of Thaxter and Loomis, and he seemed to need reassurances. It cost McQuestion nothing to oblige him.

In the morning Ravenhill accompanied him to Murray's ship, a broad-beamed, weatherbeaten old steam schooner called *The Wandering Star*. And remained on the wharf, standing morosely as the schooner steamed out across the inlet with Mc-

Question at her larboard rail. By the time *The Wandering Star* neared open sea, both Ravenhill and Skagway were dwindling specks dwarfed by the towering, barren vastness of the land he was leaving behind.

CHAPTER 12

THE TEN-DAY, TWELVE-HUNDRED-MILE trip down the Inside Passage to Seattle was uneventful and felt interminable. It was late April now, and there were no serious storms to weather. With her cargo holds empty, *The Wandering Star* made better than eight knots during the daylight hours she traveled, but to McQuestion she seemed hardly to be moving at all. And each night from dark to dawn, she did stand at anchor: no skipper in his right mind would have tried navigating these unchartered and unlighted waters by night, Murray told him, and the captain was an old hand at the Alaska trade.

The schooner was a tramp commercial freebooter that had plied most of the seven seas and spent the past six months shuttling between Seattle and Skagway, carrying gold hunters and supplies.

Carrying several hundred head of cattle last trip, along with a bunch of Oregon cowboys who planned to take the beeves into the Yukon by the inland route from Pyramid Harbor, near Skagway, and then raft them down the Yukon River to Dawson after breakup and sell them to the meat-hungry sourdoughs.

"Turned my ship into a goddamn cattle boat," Murray said. "I don't know why I let them crazy bastards talk me into it."

But the cowboys weren't so crazy at that, McQuestion thought. Their plan was a risky one, but it could be done. And if they succeeded with minimum losses, it would probably make them wealthier than any of the thousands of damn-fool stampeders with their dreams of gold.

The Wandering Star smelled richly of the cattle, and of copra, whale oil, herring, and the other cargoes she'd carried over the years. But she was well kept: Murray ran a tight ship. Her decks were clean, her rigging, sail, guy lines, and deck gear were all in top condition, and her broad funnel gleamed with fresh paint. The crew, because of the way the captain worked them, was a sullen bunch that kept to themselves. Except for meals and an occasional game of cribbage with Murray and his first mate, McQuestion spent his time alone on deck or in his cabin. He was the only passenger.

He preferred it that way, yet the inactivity, the

waiting, tried his patience nonetheless. The first mate was a literate man and loaned him some of the books from his private library: Headley's *Heroes and Battles of the Civil War*, Esquemeling's *The Buccaneers of America*, a volume of stories about a detective named Sherlock Holmes. He read until his eyes ached with strain. Paced the deck restlessly for hours on end. Slept too little and thought too much.

One of the thoughts that occupied him, something he hadn't let himself think much about before, was the consequences of what he was doing, the price he might have to pay. By playing a lone hand, he had directly disobeyed Colonel Steele's orders and broken other regulations as well. Now, away from Canadian soil, he no longer had jurisdiction as a law officer. He could seek help from United States authorities, of course, but this was something he wouldn't do until he caught his quarry, or unless it was absolutely necessary in order to take them into custody. He had no papers authorizing him to act on behalf of the Crown. Ottawa might grant him status as an official representative of the Force if he explained the situation to their satisfaction, but then again they might not; and even if they did, the trail of Thaxter and Loomis might be so cold by the time it came that he'd never find them. No, he was committed to playing his lone hand through to the end. Once he captured the two fugitives, *then* he could proceed according to the manual and attempt to make peace with Colonel Steele and Ottawa.

Not that that would be easy. Steele was a stickler for discipline, and so was Ottawa. McQuestion remembered the colonel's words at division headquarters: "If at any time you find yourself in a position to arrest the men responsible, you'll do so in proper accordance with regulations and with every effort to forgo violence. Otherwise, I will see to it that your career with the Force is terminated— and if necessary, that you're brought up on charges." Steele had meant what he'd said. He was not a man to make idle threats.

The one mitigating factor might be the measure of McQuestion's success. If he caught up with both Loomis and Thaxter, brought them unharmed to a representative of U.S. law to await extradition, it was possible he would get off with an official reprimand and a short suspension. Steele wasn't a compassionless man; he had to understand what was driving McQuestion in this matter. And he and his superiors believed in justice as much as McQuestion did.

But what if he failed in his hunt? McQuestion thought. What if Steele brought him up on charges in any case and he was banished from the Force? What would he do then?

These were sobering questions. He liked his work with the Mounted Police; he liked the challenge of upholding the law on the rugged Canadian frontier. Lawman and manhunter were the only positions that suited him. They had given meaning to his life after Eileen's death and his discovery that George Blanton was also dead. They defined and sustained him.

If the Force no longer wanted his services, he supposed he would return to the States and seek work as a sheriff or deputy. His father would help him find a position; even though Ben McQuestion had been retired for seven years now, he still kept in touch with old friends, men he had worked with during his days as a Dakotas lawman. There would be a job somewhere for the son of Ben McQuestion.

It was not an unappealing prospect, except for the confinement of such a position. McQuestion preferred open spaces, rough country, solitude; towns weighed on him after awhile. People, too, because of his fundamental need to keep to his own company and his own counsel. It had not always been that way, but Eileen's infidelity and death had changed him once and for all. He couldn't study law again, or love a woman in the same way again, or settle in Bismarck again. He could no longer be what he once had been.

Molly also occupied his mind. Some nights, as he walked *The Wandering Star*'s creaking deck or lay in the darkness of his cabin, he could see her face in his mind's eye as clearly as if she were there

with him. And hear again the things she'd told him
and the ghostly verses of the songs she had sung . . .

> *Fare thee well, for I must leave thee,*
> *Do not let this parting grieve thee,*
> *And remember that the best of friends*
>   *Must part . . .*

And he wondered, on those nights, if perhaps
they had lied to each other and to themselves about
the nature of their relationship. If perhaps what
they'd shared had been a kind of love after all.

Seattle surprised McQuestion, and unnerved him
somewhat. He had believed it would be a provincial
town, an inconsequential tidewater port despite the
fact that it was the outfitting center for the Klondike
rush; but what he found was a metropolis, a teeming hub of commerce. Factories and foundries, their
chimneys belching smoke into the gray afternoon
sky. The sluggish water of the harbor packed with
maneuvering freighters and other craft, shrieking
warnings at one another with sirens and bells. Huge
cargo ships berthed alongside barnacle-encrusted
wharves, tons of goods being winched up out of
their yawning hatches and then moved by hand
trucks into a long line of warehouses. And at other
wharves, at least a score of passenger steamers,
some that would be southbound to Portland and San

Francisco and other coastal ports, but the bulk of which would be traveling to Alaska: Seattle was the termini of all the competing lines on the West Coast.

When *The Wandering Star* docked just past one o'clock, McQuestion discovered that the same chaotic atmosphere reigned on shore as in Puget Sound. The wharf area was a-crawl with people, most of them, judging from their brand-new outfits, on their way to the Yukon goldfields. With dray wagons and buggies and thousands of horses, mules, oxen, sheep, and dogs. The din was tremendous: the cursing of stevedores and deck hands, the roar of winches, the bawl and howl of animals, the screech of swooping gulls, the bellow of steamship sirens. The constant Babel made McQuestion want to cover his ears. And gave him an intense longing for the desolate quiet of the wilderness.

He disembarked, carrying the grip he had bought in Skagway, and literally pushed his way off the wharves. Men who saw that he'd come off a ship just arrived from Skagway shouted questions at him, all with the word "gold" in them. He didn't answer; there was nothing he could say to people such as these.

The streets were clogged for blocks leading away from the docks. Every other store he passed seemed to be an outfitter's. The rest were cheap ho-

tels, cafes, and openly run bawdy houses. In front
of one storefront window a crowd stood staring at
something within, their faces trancelike and etched
with greed. As he shoved through, he caught a
glimpse of what held their attention: a gold nugget
about the size of a cherry, arranged on a suspended
glass tray. A placard behind it said:

KLONDIKE GOLD
A Nugget from Ten Eldorado

Ahead, a newsboy was shouting the latest bul-
letins from the goldfields—and the news, startling
to McQuestion, that war between the United States
and Spain seemed imminent. He had known that the
liberation of Cuba had become a political issue in
the States and that sentiment had been running high
against the Spanish since an unexplained explosion
had sunk the U.S. battleship *Maine* in February—
an act of Spanish sabotage, many believed. But he
hadn't considered that a declaration of war would
be the outcome.

He pressed on through the milling throngs, looking for a policeman. No one knew his town better
than a police officer; that would be the quickest and
surest way to find out where Tillie Holland had her
boardinghouse.

The first policeman he found couldn't help him,
but the second could. "Tillie Holland?" he said.

"Yes, I know her. You a friend or a relative, by any chance?"

"No," McQuestion said. "Her establishment was recommended to me."

"Well, in that case I'll tell you the truth. She's a sharp-tongued old harridan, strict as hell and particular about who she boards. If you still want to see her, knowing that, you'll find her place on Eckinshaw Road. Number twenty-one forty."

"How do I get to Eckinshaw Road?"

The policeman said it was over a mile away, near Lake Union, and told him how to get there by streetcar. The instructions were easy enough to follow; McQuestion arrived at Eckinshaw in just under half an hour.

All the residences along the 2100 block were large frame buildings, a mixture of rooming houses and private dwellings, set apart from each other and well back from the street. Trees shaded most of the front yards and porches. Tillie Holland's house was the biggest, bordered on one side by a gravel drive that led to a carriage and horse barn in the rear; rosebushes flanked the front walk in symmetrical rows. A thin woman in her sixties was sweeping the railed porch. There was nobody else around that McQuestion could see.

He went up the path. On one of the porch pillars was a neatly painted sign reading ROOMS FOR RENT. Below it, in smaller letters, were the words

NO LOGGERS, SAILORS, OR SALESMEN NEED APPLY. The policeman's assessment of Tillie Holland, it seemed, had been an accurate one.

The woman stopped sweeping as McQuestion approached. He took off his hat and said, "Excuse me, ma'am. Would you be Mrs. Holland?"

She gave him an appraising look and then smiled. "Land sakes, no," she said. "I'm Mrs. Broadhurst. One of the boarders here. I help out with the chores when I can, as a favor to Tillie."

"She's not here right now, I take it?"

"No, she's gone shopping. Are you interested in a room?"

"Actually, I'm looking for a relative of Mrs. Holland's, just down from the Yukon—a man named Floyd Loomis. I understand he might be staying here."

"Why yes, he is. Mr. Loomis is Tillie's nephew."

"May I ask when he arrived?"

"Yesterday morning. He and his partner are together. They had quite a difficult time up North, you know. Lost everything. Did you just come from the Yukon yourself, young man?"

"Yes, ma'am. Would Mr. Loomis's partner's name be William Thaxter?"

"It would," Mrs. Broadhurst said. "A pleasant young fellow, very polite. The same as you, I may say."

"Thank you. Mrs. Holland put them both up on the first floor, did she?"

"The first floor? Why no, on the second floor. Two of her best rooms at the rear, eleven and twelve. They get the morning sun, you know."

McQuestion nodded "Would Mr. Loomis and Mr. Thaxter be in their rooms now?"

"Well, I don't rightly know. I haven't seen either of them since yesterday, come to think of it. I can run in and find out, if you'd like . . ."

"Don't trouble yourself, Mrs. Broadhurst. Now that I know for certain Mr. Loomis is rooming here, I believe I'll take the time to have a late lunch." He gave her a rueful smile. "The fact is, I haven't eaten yet today and I'm famished."

"I shouldn't wonder. There is quite a good cafe two blocks over on Green Street. Porter's, it's called."

"Thank you, ma'am."

McQuestion left her, went back to the corner, and turned it. In the middle of the block he found an alleyway, rutted except for a grassy strip in its center, that ran along the rear of the 2100-block houses. He entered the alley, not hurrying. The carriage barn he'd seen from Eckinshaw Road identified 2140 for him; the rear of the property was bordered by a low wooden fence, and in the yard beyond the barn he could see fruit trees. He could also see a set of stairs that led up the back wall of the boarding-house.

He paused for a moment to study the windows on the second floor. They were all closed and curtained; he saw no movement behind any of them. He went ahead past the barn to a gate in the fence. When he was sure both the yard and the gravel drive were empty he unlatched the gate, stepped through, and hurried across to the stairs.

The door on the second-floor landing was unlocked. He opened it, looked into a short, empty corridor, then entered. He was wearing his service revolver under the light mackinaw he'd bought in Skagway; he drew the weapon, held it up across his chest as he moved out of the ell into the main corridor.

Number eleven was the first room he came to. He edged in close to the door and stood with his ear pressed against the panel, listening. Silence. Without touching the porcelain knob, he went along to number twelve adjacent and listened there. More silence.

McQuestion stood for a moment, debating. Then he put the fingers of his left hand on the knob, turned it slowly, found it unlocked, and shoved the door open. This room was empty. In fact, it seemed to have hardly been occupied. The bed quilt was rumpled but the bed had not been slept in. There were no personal belongings in sight, no sign of luggage of any type.

He pulled the door shut, retraced his steps to number eleven. That door was also unlocked, he found—but when he had it open, the room beyond proved not to be empty. McQuestion stood on the threshold, staring in at the bed, and in his stomach there was a queer, sick feeling. The sudden anger that welled up was bitter and a little wild.

His search for Floyd Loomis had finally come to an end. But it wasn't at all the end he had expected or the kind that he could ever abide.

Loomis lay sprawled across the bed, blood-spattered, dead, with the handle of a skinning knife protruding from the side of his scrawny neck.

CHAPTER 13

A series of low thumping sounds made McQuestion jerk his head around: someone was coming up the inside stairs. He ducked into the room, eased the door shut, leaned against it. Footsteps sounded in the hallway, but they did not turn in his direction; he heard them fade, finally stop altogether. A few seconds later a door slammed distantly.

Just one of the boarders coming home, he thought. He let out the breath he'd been holding, holstered his pistol, and swung around to the bed. From the looks of the body and the blood dried on it, Loomis had been dead a long while—since some time last night, probably. He was fully dressed except for one boot that had been cast off to the floor. There were small indications of a struggle: the chamber pot had been kicked out from under the bed, the lampshade had been knocked awry, a water pitcher lay on its side on the nightstand and the corner of the bed beneath it was wet from spillage.

McQuestion scanned the rest of the room. A duffel bag sat on the one chair, drawn open so that a jumble of clothing was visible inside. He moved over to the bag and fingered through its contents. Clothing, a few minor personal possessions, an Elks lodge button with the words LEWISTON, IDAHO on it, an empty buckskin knife sheath that told him the murder weapon had belonged to Loomis. That was all.

When he turned again to face the bed, something on the carpet near one of the posts caught his attention. He knelt there, put his face close to the nap, and found a couple of grains of gold dust. A quick search of the rest of the carpeting turned up more particles. It looked as though part of a poke had been spilled and the dust hastily retrieved.

Was that the motive for the killing—gold? The two of them could have held out on Ravenhill, could have come away from the Yukon with a few hundred dollars' worth of dust. Perhaps Loomis had tried to steal Thaxter's share. Or perhaps Loomis had held out on Thaxter and Thaxter had caught him, lost his temper, and used the knife.

Well, that was unimportant right now. The important things were that Loomis was dead and Thaxter was still at large. The proper procedure was to report the murder to the Seattle authorities; but if he did that, he would have to explain why he had entered the boardinghouse illegally. The local police might decide to detain him, and Thaxter had enough of a jump on him as it was—still close to a full day.

But a jump to where? Thaxter wouldn't have stayed in Seattle. He was as much of a coward as Loomis had been when he felt threatened or unsure of himself. The way he'd turned tail and fled the Yukon proved that. No, he'd have left the city as soon as he was able. Stagecoach, horseback, train, steamship—too damned many means of travel.

His destination had to depend at least in part on whether or not he had friends here in the Northwest, someplace to settle in for a while. Lewiston, Idaho, for instance . . . apparently that was Loomis's hometown. If Thaxter didn't have friends in the area, then it was a good bet he'd head home to California . . .

McQuestion had spent enough time in this room. He went to the door, listened, then opened it a crack and peered into the hallway. Empty. He slipped out, entered number twelve, and searched that room quickly. But there was nothing to find. Thaxter had left no clues to where he might have gone.

Walking soft, McQuestion went back along the hallway to the ell. Through the rear-door glass he could see a wagon clattering past in the alley; he waited until it was gone before he stepped onto the landing. A woman was hanging wash in one of the yards opposite, but she had her back to him. And she didn't turn as he came down the stairs and hurried out the gate.

Three blocks away, he boarded the same-number streetcar that had brought him here and rode it downtown. He left the car at Pioneer Place and made his way back to the docks, where another policeman provided directions to the various steamship company offices. McQuestion still carried the torn photograph of William Thaxter he had found in the abandoned Indian River cabin; if Thaxter had left Seattle by steamer last night or this morning, he might have used an assumed name this time but the clerk who'd sold him the ticket ought to remember him. If he hadn't taken a steamer, the railroad offices would be McQuestion's next stop. And after that, the stage lines, liveries, and horse brokers.

But it did not come to that. The balding clerk at the third place he tried, the Pacific Coast Steamship Company, squinted at the photograph through his eyeglasses and said, "Gent looks familiar, all right. He came in first thing this morning, if I'm not mistaken."

"Where was he bound?"

"San Francisco."

"Which ship did he leave on?"

"*The Humboldt Lady*. Departed eight A.M. on the dot."

"And what name did he give?"

"Well, let's see," the clerk said. He cudgeled his memory briefly, shrugged, and shuffled through a file of papers until he came up with a passenger list. "Here we are. Oh yes—McQuestion, that was the name. Mr. Z. McQuestion."

"What!"

"Yes, sir. Odd name, isn't it? I don't recall that I've seen it before."

"I have," McQuestion said thinly. "When is your next ship for San Francisco?"

"Tomorrow morning, eight A.M. The *Eureka*, pride of the line."

"Would you know if any of the other companies have a sailing scheduled for tonight?"

The question ruffled the clerk's sense of propriety. In a stiff voice he said, "The earliest boat out is the *Eureka*, tomorrow morning, and none finer on the San Francisco run, either. Would you care to purchase a ticket, sir?"

McQuestion bought cabin passage, paid for his ticket, and went outside. A light rain had begun to fall and the sky was dark, angry-looking. It matched his mood. He was seething inside.

On top of everything else the son of a bitch had stolen his *name*!

He ate a tasteless supper at a restaurant on Yesler

Way, on the edge of the city's tenderloin, then took a room for the night in a cheap hotel nearby, paying an outrageous price for the privilege of sleeping on a cot with a lice-ridden mattress and a tattered blanket. He was up before dawn, shaved, and on the street at first light. It had rained throughout the night—the streets glistened wetly under the pale flicker of the gas lamps—but the clouds were breaking up now. Compared to what he had been used to in the Yukon, the wind blowing in off the harbor was almost warm.

As early as it was, crowds were already gathering in the wharf area. The waterfront itself was teeming with Northbound gold seekers, teamsters, sailors; drays and baggage vans; and more strings of animals consigned to Skagway and Dyea for the deadly mountainous trek into the Yukon. Again, McQuestion was assaulted by the noise level. And again he felt a longing for the solitude of the frontier.

He made his way to the Colman Wharf, where the *Eureka* was berthed. She was a fine-looking ship; McQuestion estimated her at better than three hundred feet in length and upward of two thousand tons gross. One of the fast coastwise flyers, carrying general cargo and passengers between San Francisco and Seattle, with limited service to the smaller ports in between. He wondered if the steamer Thaxter had taken, *The Humboldt Lady*, was also a flyer. If not, if she was one of the smaller packets that made numerous shuttle stops, there was a chance the *Eureka* would reach San Francisco Bay ahead of her. He would ask the purser about that first thing after he boarded.

On his way to the gangplank, he passed a drawn-up wagon containing a pair of steamer trunks and some smaller pieces of luggage. The driver, a heavy-set, mean-looking fellow with too much belly, was engaged in an argument with one of two young women. The woman was dark, slim, comely in a blue serge traveling skirt, a light jacket over a frilly white waist, and a small hat with a raised veil. Her companion was younger by five or six years, no more than twenty, equally attractive but pale and skittish-looking. She wore similar clothing, but at least one size too large for her.

"How can you stand there and lie to my face like this?" the older woman was saying. She was angry; two spots of crimson, like circles of heavily applied rouge, colored her cheeks. "The price you quoted my sister and me was two dollars. *Two* dollars, my good man, not three."

"The hell it was, lady."

"And I'll thank you not to use profanity."

"I'll thank *you* to pay me what you owe me. I ain't got all day to stand around here and pussyfoot with you. Pay up or I don't unload your gear."

"Two dollars, not a penny more."

"Three dollars, I said. Now pay up, little lady, and be quick about it."

There was something about the argument that had made McQuestion tarry and listen in. He watched the older sister hand the drayman two one-dollar bills. The man looked at them, folded them in half, tucked them into his shirt pocket, glared at the woman, and deliberately spat onto the planks near his off horse.

"One dollar more," he said.

"I told you, you'll not get another penny—"

"One dollar more, goddamn it!"

The younger sister began to cry; the other one put an arm around her shoulders, said something soothing to her, and glared back at the teamster. McQuestion was moving before he realized it. He came up alongside the older sister and said to her, "Pardon me, miss. Some trouble here?"

"None that concerns you," the teamster said belligerently.

McQuestion ignored him, still looking at the woman. She said, "This person quoted us a price of two dollars at our hotel to deliver and unload our luggage. Now he demands three dollars or he won't unload."

"In that case," McQuestion said, "I'll be glad to unload your luggage for you myself."

"The hell you will, mister," the teamster said. "You stay away from my wagon."

McQuestion continued to ignore him. He moved to the rear of the dray, reached in to grasp the handle on one of the steamer trunks. The drayman cursed angrily, came bulling up to him, and launched a flat-handed blow toward McQuestion's upper body, with the intention of knocking him aside. McQuestion blocked it with his left forearm, stepped forward, and jabbed the knuckles of his right hand into the teamster's chest, just under the heart. The man's breath spilled out in a whooshing grunt; his eyes popped, his face turned a mottled red. He sat down on the dock and began to groan.

McQuestion said to the two sisters, "I'm sorry, ladies. But he gave me no choice."

"Of course he didn't," the older one said approvingly. Her sister was still sniffling; she seemed preoccupied and a little ill. "He had it coming to him."

"So he did." McQuestion dragged the two trunks out of the dray, set them on the planking, and placed the other bags on top of them. The teamster was still sitting near his off horse with his legs splayed out in front of him, struggling to regain his breath. He no longer looked bellicose; as with most bullies, one sharp blow had taken all the fight out of him.

"My name is Della Longwell," the older woman said. Her eyes, McQuestion noticed, were dark brown and frankly appraising of him. "This is my sister, Jody."

"My pleasure, ladies," he said, and introduced himself.

"Are you sailing on the *Eureka*, Mr. McQuestion?"

"I am."

"Well then, we'll be shipmates. Jody and I are on our way to visit relatives in San Francisco. We're from Montana—Helena."

"A fine town, Helena."

"You know it? Yes, it's a fine town." Her expression darkened briefly, as if an unpleasant memory had passed across her mind. Then it was gone and she smiled again. "Do you live in Seattle, Mr. McQuestion?"

"No. I'm from the Yukon."

"Oh! You're a prospector, then?"

He smiled and did not deny it. If he told her the truth, she would only ask questions he had no desire to answer.

Jody Longwell plucked at the sleeve of her sister's jacket. "Della, could we go aboard?" she said in a small, pale voice. "I'm not feeling very well."

"Of course, dear." Della's face had darkened again; she took Jody's arm. But her eyes lingered on McQuestion, as if she were somewhat reluctant to end their conversation. "Perhaps we will see each other during the voyage, Mr. McQuestion."

"Perhaps we will. You and your sister go ahead,

Miss Longwell. I'll see that your baggage is put aboard."

"Thank you." She gave him another smile, nodded, and led Jody away to the gangplank.

McQuestion watched after them for a moment. The Longwell sisters had problems too, he thought. But just what they were were none of his concern. And women, even one as attractive as Della Longwell, had no place in his life right now. No place at all.

The *Eureka*'s whistle echoed shrilly. He shrugged, summoned one of the ship's porters to accommodate the ladies' luggage, and went on board to talk to the purser.

The Humboldt Lady, he was told, was also a fast coastwise flyer; there was no way the *Eureka* would be able to beat or cut her time to San Francisco. Thaxter would still have a twenty-four-hour lead on him when he arrived.

CHAPTER 14

DESPITE HIS VOW to the contrary, McQuestion found himself spending a good deal of time with Della Longwell on the voyage south.

She sought him out the first night, before supper, and sat at table with him. She invited him to play whist with her and two other passengers, and when he said he didn't know the game, she suggested others and finally talked him into a two-handed game of cribbage. She asked him to call her Della, began calling him Zack. It was plain she had taken a fancy to him. Some women would have been coy or merely flirtatious; Della was frank, straightforward, the sort of level-headed woman McQuestion had always admired.

Her persistence annoyed him at first. But she *was* attractive—dark brown hair that had a silky sheen to it, a more than ample bosom, long-fingered, expressive hands—and not at all an unpleasant companion and conversationalist. She seemed determined to be cheerful, for her sister's sake as well as her own and McQuestion's. He saw nothing more of Jody Longwell, though; Della told him Jody was prone to seasickness, no matter what the weather happened to be, and was keeping to their cabin for that reason. He thought this was at least partly a lie, but he did not press her about it.

Other information about herself and her sister, Della volunteered freely. Their father had been a lawyer in Helena; he was dead two years now, of a heart attack. He had never remarried after their mother's death from smallpox when Jody was an infant, although Della, in her practical way, had urged him continually to take a second wife. There had been a fairly substantial inheritance from his estate that allowed them to live comfortably, but Della worked anyway, as a seamstress and milliner, just to keep busy. Jody's ambition was to go on the stage. Barring that, she wanted to marry well and travel to Europe and visit the Louvre and the Roman Colosseum and other such places. Fanciful dreams, of course, Della said—sadly and with a certain tragedy, McQuestion thought—but then, Jody was only twenty.

She kept probing with questions about who he was and what he did, and he finally admitted to being a North West Mounted policeman. ("A Mountie! How thrilling!" she said). But he told her only that he had business to transact in San Francisco, of a type he wasn't at liberty to discuss. And he permitted her only sketchy details of his background.

With Della for company, the days passed much more swiftly than they had on the voyage from Skagway to Seattle. For the most part he was able to keep his mind off William Thaxter and what lay ahead in California. Too much thinking was not good for any man.

On the night before they were scheduled to arrive in San Francisco—a clear spring night, surprisingly balmy for April—she asked him to walk on deck with her after supper. And as they walked, she was quieter than usual and he sensed that the silence was a prelude. There was a need in her to talk about something personal. He felt it and hoped it was nothing to do with the two of them. He liked her; he did not want to have to hurt her.

It took her a while to work up to it. When she finally did, they were standing at the larboard rail, looking out to where the moonlight laid a silvery path across the sea. She said, breaking several minutes of silence, "I suppose you're wondering just why Jody and I are going to San Francisco."

"A visit, you said."

"Yes, but not the usual sort of visit." Pause.

"You've guessed by now what ails her, haven't you?"

"It's none of my business," McQuestion said carefully. He understood what she was aiming at now, and it relieved him. He should have known that she was not one of those rash and impulsive women who threw themselves at a man after only a few days' acquaintance.

"Would you object to my confiding in you?" she asked.

"Not if it will ease your mind."

"It will. I'm not sure why; it's just that I've had it bottled up inside me for so long. And . . . well, I feel you'll understand."

McQuestion was silent, waiting.

"Jody is going to have a child, of course," Della said. "Out of wedlock."

Again McQuestion said nothing.

"She's not a bad girl, Zack. Please don't think that of her. She's just young and foolish."

"I don't think bad of her," he said. "Everyone makes mistakes, young people particularly."

"Yes. I'm taking her to San Francisco so she can have the baby without anyone back home knowing. My mother's niece lives there; and she's offered to give the child a home. She has three of her own."

"I take it the father wanted no part of marriage or parenthood?"

"No. Evan Borcher is a scoundrel." Della's voice

was angry now, full of bitterness and disgust. "He seduced Jody and tried to get her to run off with him."

McQuestion was thinking of Eileen and George Blanton; he said with bitterness of his own, "And then ran off himself when he found out she was with child, I expect."

"Not exactly. He ran off before that. With the sheriff and the United States government after him."

"Oh? What did he do, this Borcher?"

"He is a confidence man and a thief," Della said. "He swindled one of our bankers, Seth Rebway, out of more than five thousand dollars."

McQuestion frowned, turned to face her squarely. "How did he do that?"

"With forged mining stocks. He said he was a broker and he convinced Mr. Rebway that they were genuine. It didn't take long for Mr. Rebway to find out the truth, but Borcher had already left Helena by then."

"Did the sheriff catch up to him?"

"No. He disappeared. No one is sure yet how he managed it."

Dark things were stirring inside McQuestion. He was silent again.

"From the first time I laid eyes on him," Della said, "I suspected the worst. Smart and glib and sweet-talking; butter wouldn't melt in his mouth. I suppose that is what Jody saw in him. But my Lord, he's at least fifteen years older than her. And that awful scar . . ." She shuddered.

"Scar?" The word came out in a hard whisper.

"On the side of his neck. Shaped like a lightning fork."

McQuestion could feel himself trembling. Disbelief, amazement, rage, hatred—all these emotions churned within him like pieces of meat in a stewpot. It was seconds before he was able to speak again.

"What did he look like?"

"What is it, Zack? You sound strange . . ."

"Answer me. What did he look like?"

"Tall, lean. But strong. Very strong."

"His hair?"

"Black and curly."

The color was wrong. "Could it have been dyed?"

"I suppose it could have been. Zack . . ."

"Did he travel by horseback or wagon?"

"By horseback."

"What color horse?"

"A big grulla. Zack, what *is* it? Do you know Evan Borcher?"

"Not by that name. By another, maybe."

"Is he wanted by the Mounties? Is that it?"

"He's wanted, all right," McQuestion said

grimly. "How long ago was it that he disappeared from Helena?"

"A little over six weeks."

"How far was your local law able to track him?"

"As far as Bozeman. That is where he was last seen."

"Bozeman. All right," McQuestion said. "Excuse me, Della. I need some time in private."

He left her looking bewildered, before she could say anything further, and sought out the ship's saloon. He drank a shot of Canadian whiskey, carried a second to an empty table near the starboard bank of windows. The second drink helped to settle the turmoil inside him, allowed him to order his thoughts again.

Two men couldn't have so many of the same characteristics: glib-talking seducer of young women; confidence man who sold forged mining stock among his other swindles; tall, lean, strong, with curly hair and a preference for big grulla horses. And the scar . . . that was the clincher. That lightning-fork scar on the side of the neck.

Evan Borcher was George Blanton.

Blanton was *alive*!

The reality of it was stunning. Five years, five long years, he'd believed Blanton to be dead; believed that grave marker in the hillside cemetery in Moose Jaw, Saskatchewan. He had been so *sure*. The people he'd spoken to: the local constable, the undertaker, the townspeople—all of them had confirmed that the man buried there, the man who'd been found shot to death on the road, was Blanton. He remembered thinking at the time that there couldn't possibly be any mistake.

Had all those people been wrong somehow? Or had Blanton gotten to each and bribed him to tell a false story? Both explanations seemed improbable. And yet Blanton was so goddamned clever. That was how he'd stayed one stride ahead of the law all these years. He could have bribed one or two of those Moose Jaw citizens, the undertaker in particular; and he could have arranged the circumstances—shot his partner in the land swindle, planted identification on the body, phonied up that scar somehow—so that everyone else believed as McQuestion had believed.

It must have happened that way. Blanton had fooled the Canadian authorities, he'd fooled the United States authorities, he'd fooled McQuestion. And he was still out there somewhere, still cheating honest men, still seducing young girls, still destroying lives. Still free, the evil son of a bitch. Still thumbling his nose at justice.

Like William Thaxter, McQuestion thought. Only Thaxter's days were numbered; he was going to catch up to Thaxter very soon now. But who would catch up to Blanton or Borcher or whatever his real name was? Would anyone get him? Or would he keep right on swindling and destroying until he died of natural causes at a ripe old age?

McQuestion stared blindly through the saloon window. Blanton, Blanton . . . the name, the bitter knowledge that he was alive and on the loose, made his head ache. He wanted another drink; instead he shoved his chair back and left the smoky saloon, went out on deck again to let the night breeze clear his head.

And as he paced from one end of the steamer to the other, he understood that he could not allow himself to fret and stew about Blanton—not now, when he was so close to Thaxter. If he let Blanton get in the way, Thaxter might be able to elude him, might slip away as Blanton himself had done in Saskatchewan.

No, he mustn't even think about George Blanton until he settled accounts with Thaxter. Eileen had died almost six years ago; Molly had died six weeks ago. And he'd come so far, been through so much, perhaps sacrificed a great deal. Thaxter first: it *had* to be that way.

Thaxter first.

CHAPTER 15

THE *EUREKA* STEAMED through the Golden Gate toward San Francisco Bay early the following morning. It was another clear day, freshened by a light breeze; flocks of screaming gulls swooped along in their wake. On the south shore, a pair of odd tent cities had spring up—not unlike the one at Lake Bennett, although these tents were mostly gray and the installations had a military look. The ship swung south into the bay. Along the curving San Francisco waterfront were miles of docks, forests of sailing masts and steam funnels, the hulking shapes of transpacific cargo and passenger ships. The downtown skyline was strung with tall steel-frame buildings, some at least fifteen stories high.

Altogether it was an impressive sight. But McQuestion, standing at the *Eureka*'s rail, caught up in his purpose, took only superficial notice of any of it. He was impatient for the steamer to dock so he could disembark and be on his way.

Della Longwell sought him out as they passed Alcatraz Island, where the largest of the western military prisons, Fort Alcatraz, was located. She said nothing about his abrupt leave-taking of last night or his intense interest in the man she knew as Evan Borcher; she seemed to understand that it was a subject he would not discuss. Nor did she attempt to engage him in small talk. As always, she was frank and direct in what she had to say.

"Will you help me with Jody when we dock?" she asked. "She isn't well; the trip has been long and tiring for her. I'm afraid she might swoon."

McQuestion hesitated. But he couldn't find it in himself to refuse such a simple request. He agreed to help.

"Thank you, Zack. I wired our cousin from Seattle and she'll be meeting us." Della touched his arm almost shyly. "I know you have things on your mind, things you have to do in San Francisco, but . . . well, if you should find the time I'd like it very much if you would call on me."

He didn't speak.

"If you should find the time," she repeated, and pressed a slip of paper into his hand. "I've written down our cousin's address. Jody will be there at least six months, but I expect I'll return to Montana in three weeks or so, after I'm certain she will be all right."

McQuestion nodded. He had no words for her, but before she took her leave he let her see him carefully place the slip of paper inside his billfold.

He continued to stand at the rail, alone, until the *Eureka* tied up at the Howard Street wharf. Then he returned to his cabin for his grip, made his way from there to the stateroom occupied by the Longwell sisters. Jody was pale, shaky; it was necessary for him to take her elbow and support her as they left the ship. They entered the cavernous, graystone Ferry Building, where they found the cousin and two of her children. A carriage waited outside. Della's hand lingered in his as they said their goodbyes, and when the carriage rattled off through the milling waterfront crowds, she turned her head and looked back at him and waved. He forced himself to answer the wave with one of his own.

There was excitement in the crush of people, but it was not the same kind of excitement that McQuestion had felt in Seattle. It had little to do with the Yukon gold stampede; he saw only a few of the new outfits that marked the cheechako. What he felt here was the excitement caused by the coming of war.

A hundred different voices told him the general story, and the shouts of newsboys filled in the details. Only ten days before, on April 20, President

McKinley had approved a congressional resolution calling for immediate Spanish withdrawal from Cuba. Spain's response had come on April 24: she had declared war on the United States. The following day, the U.S. Congress had made it reciprocal. The Atlantic fleet had been dispatched to Cuban waters; Admiral Dewey's Asiatic Squadron was on its way to the Philippines. And McKinley had issued a call for volunteers to occupy these and other Spanish possessions in both oceans.

San Francisco, it seemed, was to become the major military assembling and shipping point for men and material needed to fight the Pacific campaign. Already newly recruited soldiers were streaming into the city, along with tons of supplies, from all over the country. Temporary camps were being set up in and around the city, the two largest on the Presidio reservation and on sand dunes out near the ocean. That explained the tent cities McQuestion had glimpsed from the deck of the *Eureka* as she passed through the Golden Gate.

There was a kind of gaiety in the war talk, a spirit of high and pleasurable adventure, that irritated him. As far as he was concerned, war was a solemn business—a condition to be avoided if at all possible, endured and ended with all dispatch if not, but never to be treated cavalierly. He had too much respect for human life, and too much personal knowledge of suffering and death, to approach the idea of war with anything except revulsion and dread. Any man who took it as sport was a damned fool.

McQuestion went back inside the Ferry Building. Ferries for Oakland, he discovered, left every thirty minutes, and one of the Southern Pacific boats was due to depart shortly. He paid a dime for a ticket and hurried on board, still carrying his grip, just before the ferry backed down from the wharf. Within the half hour it had crossed the Bay and docked again at Oakland.

He made his way up the Estuary to the Oakland City Wharf, where the ferry's purser had told him the oyster fleet put up. The place was a mixture of the colorful and the squalid: Arctic whalers, Chinese junks, Greek fishing boats, Yankee sailing ships, blackened old freighters, scows, sloops, shrimpers, oyster boats, houseboats; long rows of warehouses crowded here and there by shacks built from wreckage or from dismantled ships; and long, barren sandpits.

McQuestion approached three men to ask the whereabouts of a fisherman named Thaxter. The first two either didn't know or wouldn't say, but the third, a crusty old salt with a stocking cap pulled down over his ears, who sat propped against a piling with a half-mended fishnet across his lap, knew the name well enough. And clearly did not like it. He screwed up his face and spat off the wharfside.

"Bob Thaxter?" he said. "That who you're after, mate?"

"Unless there are any others here with that name."

"There ain't, and Christ be thanked for that."

"He's an oysterman, is he?" McQuestion asked.

"Oysterman hell! Oyster pirate, you mean."

"I didn't know that."

"Well now you do, mate. How come you're lookin' for the likes of Bob Thaxter? You ain't fixin' to join up with him, are you?"

"No. It's not him I'm looking for; it's his brother, William. You know him?"

"I do. Run off to hunt gold up North."

"That's the one."

"Same no-good bastard as Bob," the old man said. "Two of 'em worked together before all that gold fuss started. Called theirselves fishermen, but pirates is what they was and what Bob still is."

"Have you seen William lately?"

"Nope. Not in more'n a year."

"Would you know if he was back to see his brother?"

"Ain't much goes on on the waterfront I don't know," the old-timer said. "William ain't come back here. Ain't likely he will, neither."

"Why is that?"

"Some kind of trouble between him and Bob,

just before he went North. Real bad blood on Bob's part, I hear."

"You know what the trouble was?"

"Bob warn't for talkin' about it. But it was money troubles, I'll wager. Something to do with the spoils of their piratin'. Big money in that business, if a man don't care how he comes by his riches."

McQuestion nodded.

"Dirty business, I say. Oyster pirates is worse than the Chink shrimp raiders or them Greeks that poach salmon. Come June, first of the flood, they'll be a whole goddamn fleet of 'em down the Bay to Asparagus Island to set up their raidin' parties on the beds. Fish Patrol tries to stop 'em, but the bastards is too smart." The old man spat into the Bay again. "Only thing stops 'em is theirselves. Drinkin', fightin', cuttin' each other up with knives over in the sandpits. A mean scurvy lot, them boys is."

"Does Bob Thaxter keep his boat here?" McQuestion asked.

"Hell no. He wouldn't dare."

"Where, then?"

"Off Davis Wharf. He don't tie up for fear of somebody stealin' on board at night and murderin' him in his sleep."

"What's her name?"

"*Cod Catcher*. Now ain't that a laugh?"

"And he lives on board?"

"He does. Be there now, I expect. I ain't seen nor heard of him puttin' out into the Bay yet today." The old-timer gave McQuestion a sidewise look. "If you're fixin' to go out and talk to Bob, I hope you're carryin' a weapon. He ain't exactly sociable to strangers."

McQuestion ignored that. Instead he asked the whereabouts of Davis Wharf.

The old man told him; his rheumy eyes were bright. "How come you be lookin' for William, anyhow?" he asked.

"Personal reasons."

There was something in the way McQuestion spoke the words that made the old man nod and smile in a maliciously pleased way. "Why then I hope you find him, mate. I surely hope you do."

McQuestion found Davis Wharf with no difficulty. There were several sloops and schooners anchored off it, so many that he didn't waste time trying to pick out the *Cod Catcher* on his own. A ragged youth in his mid-teens, who was fishing off the wharfside with a handline, made the identification for him; the youth also agreed to rent McQuestion his own patched skiff beached in the tidal mud nearby. Unlike the old man, the boy seemed impressed that McQuestion was on his way to talk to Bob Thaxter, the oyster pirate. There was a shine in his eyes akin to hero worship. McQuestion would have liked to take him aside and shake some sense into him—but it would have been pointless. Either the youth developed sense on his own, or he grew up to be just like the man he admired. It was the way of things. You couldn't hope to make everyone walk the straight and narrow, much as you might like to try.

He stowed his grip in the skiff and rowed out to the *Cod Catcher*. She was a good-sized sloop with a small cabin amidships, her mainsail furled, her hull in need of paint but otherwise in good repair. No one was visible on deck, but from inside the cabin he could hear the discordant strumming of a banjo. He shipped his oars until he was alongside the crude jacob's ladder that had been slung over the port gunwale. He tied the skiff's painter to the ladder, drew his revolver, and climbed quickly up on deck.

The man inside heard or felt his presence; the banjo twanged and went silent, and a moment later the cabin door burst open and a bear of a man, naked to the waist, came out with a belaying pin clenched in one hand. McQuestion brought the pistol up and said, "Halt!" and the fellow pulled up short, blinking and scowling. He wore a thick black beard and his hair hung in matted ropes. The smell of whiskey and ripe body odor blew off him on the cool Bay breeze, as tangible as salt spray.

He said, "Who the hell're you?" in a voice thickened by whiskey and surprise.

"The name is McQuestion. I'm a North West Mounted policeman. Stand still, now. And drop your weapon."

The bearish man gaped at him. "You be a *what*?"

"You heard me, Thaxter. That is your name, isn't it?"

"It's my name. A Mountie? Hell, I must be drunk and dreamin' this."

"Drop your weapon, I said!"

Thaxter let the belaying pin fall clattering to the deck. He would be no mental giant in the best of circumstances, McQuestion thought; now, half drunk and caught off guard, he was completely befuddled. He pawed at his face with one hand, still gawping, his mouth open at least two inches.

"It's not you I want, Bob," McQuestion said. "It's your brother, William."

"William?"

"That's right. I've been after him for more than a month, all the way from the Yukon."

Some of the confusion cleared out of Bob Thaxter's face. "What for? What's he done?"

"Murder. William and a man named Loomis shot a woman and two Indians near Dawson City. They got clear of the Territory and took a steamer from Skagway to Seattle. After they arrived William stabbed Loomis to death in a boardinghouse."

"The hell you say!" Bob Thaxter exclaimed. He

sounded a little awed. "And he come here from Seattle, then?"

"Yes. Arrived yesterday by coastal flyer. I take it you haven't seen him?"

"William wouldn't show his face around me." Anger had crawled into the oyster pirate's eyes, dull and smoldering. "I would kill the son of a bitch and he knows it."

"Why?"

"Ain't none of your business, Mountie."

"I'm making it my business," McQuestion said. He gestured with his pistol. "What happened between you and your brother?"

Bob Thaxter hesitated. Then he said sullenly, "He stole money off'n me, that's what happened. Pret' near two thousand dollars, so's he could hie off to the Yukon and hunt for gold."

"All right, Bob. Now tell me the names of William's friends, anybody he—"

"He never had no friends."

"Perhaps not. But he knows people in this area. Who might he have gone to see when he arrived? Who might set him up with a place to stay, work of some kind, legal or illegal? He couldn't have much money with him; he'll be needing some before long."

"Nobody around like that."

"Sure, now? There must be somebody."

Bob Thaxter started to shake his head. Then he

scowled and scratched at his naked chest and said, "Kineen, maybe."

"Who would Kineen be?"

"Ben Kineen. Runs the Painted Lady in San Francisco."

"What's the Painted Lady? A boat?"

"Hell no. Deadfall on the Barbary Coast. Him and William used to be shanghai crimps when they was kids, before Kineen saved up money to open his saloon."

"Anybody else besides Kineen?"

"No. I told you, William ain't got no friends."

McQuestion gestured again with the pistol. "Bob, move over and sit down on the port gunwale."

"What for?"

"So I can watch you. I'm heading back to the wharf now and I don't want you getting any fancy ideas."

"I ain't likely to do that," Bob Thaxter said, "not with you after William. I'd row you to the wharf myself, if it helped you catch that son of a bitch."

McQuestion waited while the pirate moved over and sat on the gunwale as he'd been told. Then he backed up to the jacob's ladder, swung one leg over onto its top rung.

Bob Thaxter said, "Tell me this, Mountie: William find any gold up there in the Yukon, before him and his partner killed them folks?"

"Not much."

"I knew it. Why'd he do the murders? For *their* gold?"

"No. For their food."

The pirate gawped at him again. He didn't understand; he probably never would. Here, surrounded by an abundance of seafood, rich California produce, and foodstuffs from the Sandwich Islands and other exotic ports, the idea of murder for grub was remote and unreal. McQuestion hoped that in most places in the world that would always be the case.

He climbed down the ladder, cast off the skiff's painter, and bent to the oars. He kept his revolver within easy reach, but he had no need for it: Bob Thaxter stayed seated on the *Cod Catcher*'s gunwale until after he reached the wharf.

CHAPTER 16

IT WAS LATE afternoon when McQuestion arrived back in San Francisco. The first thing he did was to check into a small hotel on lower Market Street, near the Ferry Building, where he deposited his grip and took a few minutes to wash up. Then he asked a disapproving clerk the location of the Barbary Coast, learned that it was within walking distance, and set out into the gathering dusk.

The Barbary Coast had been famous for nearly half a century as the West's seat of sin and wickedness, as a "devil's playground" equaled by none other in the country and few anywhere in the world. Perhaps there was a good deal of truth in these widespread rumors, but McQuestion found the place tame and tawdry at this hour of the evening. He passed Cheap John clothing stores, run-down hotels and lodging houses, dance halls, deadfalls, concert saloons, expensive gambling houses, and a variety of brothels—cribs, cowyards, and parlor houses, one of the last sporting a sign that read:

MADAME LUCY
YE OLD WHORE SHOPPE

The streets were crowded: seamen, groups of young men out for a last fling before sailing off to the new war, local sports, and gay blades; gamblers, pickpockets, swindlers, and roaming prostitutes. McQuestion was propositioned half a dozen times by whores and accosted once by a bunco steerer, in the first two blocks. But for all of this, things were still quiet, almost orderly.

The center of the district seemed to be the three-block-square area between Broadway and Washington, Montgomery and Stockton streets. He found the Painted Lady saloon here, an evil-looking building down an alley off Pacific Avenue. But he didn't enter it. He wanted to know more about Ben Kineen and his operation before he did that.

He stopped into one of the fancier gambling houses on Broadway. Fresco and gilt, large paintings of voluptuous nudes, ceiling-high mirrors, dazzling lamplight; female card dealers behind long rows of mahogany tables covered in leather, on which were spread piles of greenbacks and gold and silver specie. He spent an hour there, gambling judiciously, losing no more than twenty dollars while he gained part of the information he was after. The rest of it came during another hour spent visiting some of the melodeons and other deadfalls nearby.

Ben Kineen, he learned, was one of the rougher denizens of the Barbary Coast. Until a few years ago, Kineen had run a crimping joint—a place where seamen were served doctored drinks composed of equal parts of whiskey and gin, laced with opium or laudanum or chloral hydrate, and then sold to shanghai shipmasters in need of crews. But the Sailor's Union of the Pacific had put an end to that, forcing the corrupt city government to close the Painted Lady temporarily. When it reopened it was as a simple deadfall where customers were relieved of their money by "pretty waiter girls," bunco ploys, rigged games of chance, and the use of knockout drops only when all else failed.

There had been three known murders in the Painted Lady, and any number of unknown ones; corpses were common enough in the nearby alleys. Brawls were much more common. But Kineen himself remained aloof from it all. He employed bouncers as well as whores and assorted cutthroats and disappeared into his office at the rear whenever trouble broke out. It wasn't that he was a coward— he was said to be a strapping man, with mustaches waxed to points, who had been in his share of fist-fights and cutting scrapes. It was just that he considered himself above such rowdiness these days: he had aspirations to own a better class of saloon in a more respectable neighborhood and spent his free time consorting with middle-class merchants and professional men who either didn't know or chose to overlook his Barbary Coast background.

Each midnight he left the Painted Lady in the company of a bodyguard and walked to his house on Union Street near Washington Square—a ritual from which he seldom deviated. The bodyguard would bid him good-night at the front gate. Kineen's fierce reputation, and the commonly known fact that he never carried more than a few dollars, made the bodyguard a mere affectation. He had never been accosted on his nightly stroll home.

McQuestion walked back to the Painted Lady, through streets that were crowded now, much rowdier, gaudy with splashes of red and yellow lamplight, noisy with the beat of pianos and the twang of fiddles and banjos. This time he entered the deadfall. He did not expect to find William Thaxter here, but just the same he scanned the raucous crowd carefully from under the pulled-down brim of his hat. He saw no familiar faces. But he did see Ben Kineen—confirming the identification by asking one of the powdered and rouged waiter girls.

Kineen was lodged inside a barred cashier's cage

as impregnable-looking as any bank's. He was sweating, red-faced, gone to fat around the middle of his heavy frame; the waxed points of his mustache glistened in the smoky light. He wore a brocade vest with an elk's tooth chain across the front, a black cutaway coat, and a high collar. From a distance he resembled a somewhat pompous banker. But from three feet away, which was as close as McQuestion could get without making himself conspicuous, there was a greedy shine in Kineen's eyes, and the marks of his rough, brawling past were plain to see.

McQuestion left shortly, made his way out of the Barbary Coast past Portsmouth Square, and took his dinner at an oyster house on Market Street. At his hotel he tipped one of the bellboys twenty-five cents to come rapping on his door at half after eleven. Then he went upstairs, lay down on the bed in his room and allowed his tired body and mind a few hours' rest.

He was already awake and pulling on his boots when the bellboy knocked. He put on his mackinaw, adjusting it over the holstered revolver, and proceeded downstairs. There was a city map at the desk; he consulted it, fixing street names and locations in his mind.

Outside it was cooler now, almost chilly. Thin wisps of fog curled around the Ferry Building's tall clock tower, around the fifteen-story giants farther uptown. In the distance, over the clanging of cable-car bells, he could hear the faint, deep-throated call of foghorns.

He went down along the waterfront, moving parallel to the edge of the Barbary Coast until he reached the district called North Beach. He found Union Street with no trouble. Ben Kineen's house, according to what he had learned on his rounds earlier, was on the north corner of Union and Bannam Place. When he neared it he saw that it was a smallish Victorian with a front yard enclosed by a black iron picket fence; the yard was choked with shrubbery and cypress hedges that grew in close to an outside staircase. No light showed in any of the house's windows. And the nearest gas lamp was on the opposite corner, so that none of its pale, shimmery glow reached into Kineen's yard.

McQuestion moved over under the gas lamp and paused there to read his old stem-winder. Ten past midnight. The sidewalks were deserted as far as he could see; the nearest sign of life was two blocks down Union, where a lamplit carriage was clattering through the misty intersection.

He recrossed the street, glancing at the houses neighboring Kineen's. Only one of them showed light, and that in a window facing the street. He walked directly to Kineen's gate, opened it, slipped inside, and blended into the shadows alongside the cypress hedges.

The front pathway hooked away at the foot of the stairs, around the east side of the house. McQuestion followed it to the rear of the property—into another yard, this one less overgrown and enclosed by a board fence, with a shed and a stack of lumber abutting it. The house's rear windows were as dark as those in front, although he spied that one of them on the second floor was open partway. Carelessness on Kineen's part, perhaps. Or an indication that someone who craved fresh air was asleep in that room.

He returned to the front, moving slowly and silently, and took a position on one knee near the foot of the stairs, in the heavy darkness behind the hedge growing there. He was certain that he could not be seen from the street. Nor even from the pathway or the lower half of the staircase. But by parting the cypress branches, he could see out well enough.

It was no more than ten minutes before two men appeared on Union Street, approaching from the direction of the Barbary Coast. McQuestion tensed as they drew closer and finally halted before Kineen's gate. Their faces were shadowed, but he could hear them clearly when they spoke their good-nights. Kineen and his bodyguard. He hadn't expected Thaxter to come home with Kineen—to find his quarry that easily—but the possibility had strayed through his mind nonetheless.

Kineen opened the gate and came inside; the bodyguard continued on down the block. McQuestion drew his revolver. He waited until Kineen reached the staircase and put his foot on the first tread, then thumbed the pistol's hammer to cock. The click was loud in the stillness—and no man who has heard it before could ever mistake it for anything else. Kineen sucked in his breath, went rigid with his head twisting toward the hedge.

"Stand where you are, Ben Kineen," McQuestion said softly. "Cry out or make any movement, I'll shoot you dead."

Kineen believed it. He stood still, squinting, trying to see through the hedge into the darkness beyond. Fifteen or twenty seconds of heavy silence passed. The bodyguard was out of sight now, having turned the corner at the next intersection and been swallowed by the night mist.

"If you're after money and valuables, footpad, you've picked the wrong victim," Kineen said. His surprise had worn off now; he sounded puzzled and angry, but not fearful. "I've nothing but a ten-dollar gold piece and a two-dollar pocket watch."

"I'm not a footpad," McQuestion said. "And I'm not after your valuables."

"Then what—?"

"Come around here, slowly. Walk until I tell you to stop, and keep your eyes front."

The saloon owner hesitated. But when McQuestion uncocked the pistol and then thumbed its hammer again, making a second audible click, Kineen did as he'd been told. He tried to see McQuestion's face as he passed the hedge, but McQuestion kept his head ducked and in shadow.

McQuestion let him get five paces farther along the path. Then he said, "That's far enough," and stood up and moved out behind him.

Kineen said, "What now?"

"Now you answer some questions. How many people inside your house?"

No response.

"How many, Kineen? Answer me."

"Just my woman, is all."

"Upstairs, rear bedroom?"

"That's right."

"No boarders or house guests?"

"None. Listen here, my friend—"

"I am not your friend," McQuestion said. "I'm looking for William Thaxter; he's your friend. Tell me if you've seen him yesterday or today."

Silence for a few seconds. Then, "Why?"

"Answer the question."

"You're a grudge after William, is that it?"

"I'm waiting, Kineen."

"Well, it's nothing to me. I saw him. He came to talk to me yesterday afternoon."

"Where? At the Painted Lady?"

"You seem to know a hell of a lot about my affairs, mister. Just who are you?"

"Did Thaxter come to your saloon?"

". . . He did."

"What did he want?"

"The loan of a hundred dollars and a job. I gave him neither one."

"Why not?"

"I am not a moneylender," Kineen said. "I don't make loans—not to gents I knew in my wayward days, not even to my own kin. And I have more hired help than I need."

"How did Thaxter take to your refusal?"

"He kept pestering me. I told him to go to his brother; he said he couldn't do that because they had had a falling out. So I got rid of him another way."

"What way?"

"I suggested he look up Hester Coolidge—Hester Thompson, as he knew her. Her husband died a few weeks ago; their farm in Petaluma belongs to her now. They had no children."

"Thaxter used to know this Hester, did he?"

"As well as a man and a woman can know each other," Kineen said. "But he boxed her around and she wouldn't stand for it. She ran off and married Coolidge five years ago."

"How do you know so much about her?"

"Hester's cousin works for me and she likes to talk."

"What did Thaxter say when you told him?"

"He said a farm in Petaluma sounded good to him. He had the notion he could square himself with Hester."

"So that's where he went, then—to Petaluma?"

"Yes."

"Where is that?"

"About forty miles due north of here."

"Big place or a little one?"

"Little. Population of two or three thousand."

"Who else lives on Hester Coolidge's farm?"

"Just her, as far as I know."

McQuestion said, "Well and good, Kineen. You've been very helpful. Now walk on ahead."

"To where?"

"The shed in back. And no arguments."

Again Kineen obeyed. When they got to the shed McQuestion ordered him to open the door and walk inside without turning around. Kineen did that— and McQuestion caught hold of the door and pushed it shut between them.

From inside Kineen said, "If I ever find out who you are, mister, you'll pay for this. You'll pay dear."

McQuestion didn't answer. He picked up a length of cut board from the stack nearby and wedged it at an angle between the door latch and the ground. Then he hurried back around to the front yard.

Kineen began to fuss inside the shed, banging on the door and yelling, but McQuestion was half a block away on Union Street before window sashes went up and the first lamp was lit.

CHAPTER 17

AN HOUR PAST dawn McQuestion took a ferry to Sausalito and then boarded a San Francisco and North Pacific Railroad train for Petaluma. It was the fastest way to get to the town. There was a more direct route, via paddle-wheel steamer across San Pablo Bay and up an estuary called Petaluma Creek, but the first boat out wasn't until late morning.

On the train, he shared a seat with an undersized drummer of drug sundries. ("Everything from female-complaint medicine to prophylactics," the little man said confidentially, tapping his sample case.) The drummer, as gregarious as most of his breed, had spent twenty years traveling the counties north of San Francisco; when he learned that McQuestion was a stranger in the area and headed for

Petaluma, he offered a fount of local anecdotes and historical detail. McQuestion paid attention to some of it, asking questions now and then, because he liked having as much information about an unfamiliar place as he could get before entering it.

Petaluma was an agricultural town, for the most part—poultry, eggs, feed and grain, alfalfa, a few other crops. Eggs were its primary industry; more than half the eggs shipped to San Francisco from the entire state were from Petaluma. It had better than fifty saloons—"drinking hells," the drummer called them, and added unnecessarily that he himself was a temperance man—and the nearby hills were "riddled with bootlegging stills." There was a city jail and a small peace-keeping force, but the town was "mostly a respectable place. Haven't been but half a dozen murders and one hanging in Petaluma since it was incorporated."

The drummer didn't know where the Coolidge farm was. He did know that a good horse could be rented at Elford's Livery on Main Street above Steamer Basin and that the telegraph office was on Main, the city jail was on Fourth, and the police chief's name was Canfield. And if McQuestion was interested in "letting his hair down some," why, there was a spot out near a place called The Haystacks that was run by a right friendly widow woman . . .

The time passed swiftly enough, with the drummer's voice droning on. McQuestion was able to keep the waiting and the inactivity from knotting him up inside. But he was on his feet as soon as the train whistled down for the Petaluma station, interrupting one of the drummer's monologues with a hasty word of parting. When the locomotive hissed to a stop he was the first passenger off the cars.

It was warm here, the air thick with the summery smells of dust and growing things and with the stench of hot oil from the train. Green foothills stretched out to the east, beyond miles of open farmland. To the west he could see the brown line of the estuary and the town proper fanned along its far bank.

He boarded a horse-drawn cable car that took him across the estuary to Main Street. Elford's Livery was a four-block walk and turned out to be situated opposite a city park where a military detachment was recruiting local boys for the war effort; McQuestion could hear a lieutenant with a megaphone promising them a chance to join Theodore Roosevelt's crack band of Rough Riders. But the walk was worth McQuestion's time. The hostler not only had a good horse for hire—a lean and sturdy claybank—but he knew the Coolidges and was willing to share his knowledge without prying into McQuestion's reasons for asking.

"Sam and me were friends," he said. "I used to go out to his place all the time to play euchre. Fine man, Sam. Shocked me when I heard he died. Caught the grippe and it turned to pneumonia just about overnight, Doc Harmon says."

"How has Mrs. Coolidge been bearing up?"

"Better than you'd expect. First all the troubles they had with the farm, then Sam up and dying so sudden. Plenty of women would've took to their beds. But Miz Coolidge, she's a strong one."

"Is she still living at the farm?"

The hostler nodded. "Wouldn't hear of moving into town, even for a while. Said she didn't want to put nobody out."

"Does she have hired hands to help her with the chores, at least?"

"Hired hands? No, sir, nobody a-tall. Sam had to let their last hired man go two months ago."

"You spoke of troubles with the farm, Mr. Elford. What sort of troubles?"

"Whole string of 'em. Been real dry around here for a year now, and they had poor crops. Then their well went bad. Then the barn caught fire and burned right down to the ground. Some folks been saying the place is jinxed, but I don't hold with that kind of talk."

"What crops have the Coolidges been raising?"

"Alfalfa, mostly. Got a hundred or so laying hens, and a good thing, too. I reckon Miz Coolidge would've about starved by now, otherwise. She's purely set against accepting charity of any kind, and that includes food."

"So it has never been a wealthy farm?"

"Lord no. Sam had to struggle all his life to make a decent living. Hard work's one of the things that shortened his life, I'd say."

"I see. How do I get there, Mr. Elford?"

"Well, it's about four mile out Oak Creek Road," Elford said. "Easy enough to find." He went on to give directions to Oak Creek Road, and described a landmark that would identify the wagon trail leading in to the Coolidge farm.

McQuestion thanked him, paid in advance for the claybank, and left his grip in the hostler's care. He rode out of town to the north, following Elford's directions. The claybank was spirited and wanted to run; McQuestion held him down for a while, because it had been better than half a year since he'd sat a saddle and the one Elford had given him was stiff and of an unfamiliar design. But he was used to it by the time he reached the cutoff for Oak Creek Road and he gave the horse his head, letting him sprint for a mile or so before hauling him down again.

The road wound through rich farmland, much too fallow and dry-looking for this time of year. The water in the creek paralleling the road was nothing more than a trickle. It had been a long dry spell here, all right.

The day was hot. A farm wagon passed him once, churning up dust; the only other people he saw were men working here and there in the fields. He stopped briefly at the creek to water the clay-bank and rinse his own mouth. The muscles all through his upper body were corded now, so that he rode stiff-backed, like a fundamentalist preacher.

Don't think about Thaxter. If he's there, let it happen the way it will.

The landmark the hostler had told him about—a lightning-struck live oak—appeared ahead. Mc-Question slowed the claybank. The rutted wagon trail was visible beyond the tree, angling away across a short meadow; but a low, grassy hill hid the farm from the road. That was fine. He wanted a look at the place from a safe distance before he went near it, and that hill might do. There was cover along its brow: more live oaks and some bare rocks jutting up through the grass.

He turned onto the trail, but left it after a short distance and walked the horse across the meadow and up along the backbone of the hill. Near the crown he dismounted, ground-reined the claybank, and moved up among the rocks to where he could see what lay on the far side.

The farm was there, tucked up in a little valley, flanked on two sides by alfalfa fields. From where he stood, the farm buildings were better than three hundred yards away. He could see a bunch of white and brown hens moving behind chicken-wire fencing, a couple of horses grazing inside a pole corral with a lean-to shelter at the near end. But there was no sign of Thaxter or the woman Hester.

The farm had a gone-to-seed look. Both the farmhouse and the chicken coop were in need of whitewash; the remains of the burned-out barn still sat off to one side, all but one wall collapsed into rubble and that leaning like a collection of fire-blackened bones; the small windmill had lost two of its blades; the vegetable patch on the near side of the house was full of weeds and barren plants and vines. The fields, too, were in poor condition: they hadn't been plowed for the spring planting and sprouted weeds and thistles.

A place that was dying, McQuestion thought. A place that would be dead in another few months, if someone didn't take it in hand. There was something sad and lonely about it—a blighted, tragic place. The only sound that came from it, just audible in the stillness, was the irregular, ratchety rhythm of the windmill's remaining blades turning in the afternoon breeze. Like the beat of a bad heart. Like the beginnings of a death rattle.

William Thaxter had expected to find rich land here, just as he'd expected to find it in the Yukon; and he'd been disillusioned and defeated again. It couldn't have set well with him. Had he stayed away, because of the woman? Or had he moved on again, to prolong the hunt? Either way, McQuestion would know the answer soon.

Another thought crossed his mind. The hostler, Elford, had told him that Hester Coolidge might have starved by now if it weren't for the chickens. If Thaxter *was* down there with her, he couldn't have had much to eat since his arrival. That was fitting, too. He'd fled two thousand miles from the Yukon and the hunger that had led him to commit four cold-blooded murders, and he had gained nothing. He had exchanged one starvation camp for another . . .

McQuestion studied the surrounding terrain. The hill he was on spread out to the south, sloping down gradually to a shallow gully where the creek flowed. The gully ran along two hundred yards or so to the rear of the farm buildings, through humped-up meadowland and a stand of willows. To the west, beyond the untilled alfalfa fields, the land rose again into a series of short, rolling hillocks. There was no cover over that way; none anywhere within a fifty-yard radius of the buildings. The only way to make his approach was on a diagonal from the rear, from where this hill leveled out at the gully—and that meant crossing those two hundred yards of open ground to either the chicken coop or the burned-out barn.

Don't think about it. Just get it done.

He backed down below the crown of the hill and

went laterally along its backbone, descending toward the gully. When he reached it he followed its westward progress to where a lone willow drooped its branches down over the bank. He stopped there because he could see the farm buildings again. Still no sign of anyone out and around.

He followed the gully a ways further, running now, bent low to the ground, then cut away from it across the rocky meadow. His revolver was in his hand, held down along his right leg. He kept his eyes up as he ran, watching the farmhouse; the sun glinted off the glass in its rear windows, so he couldn't see if anyone was there. But the back door stayed shut and the farmyard stayed empty.

The chicken coop was the closest building; he ran on a veer toward it, until he put the coop between himself and the house. When he reached its back wall he eased along it and around on the far side, along the chicken-wire fencing in front. Some of the hens scratching inside the yard set up a minor squawking, but it wasn't enough to alert anybody in the house. He kept on going, at an angle through the vegetable patch, still watching the backside of the house. He could see into the windows now, past faded curtains. All of them were empty.

Dry cornstalks crunched under his feet; he sidestepped onto clear ground, slowing, using his free hand to rub away runnels of sweat that stung his eyes. The back stairs were straight ahead, but he bypassed them, went to the near corner and along the side wall instead. He was not going to blunder inside, not without knowing if Thaxter was here or what the situation was.

Toward the front was a window, its sash raised a few inches. He stopped alongside it and half squatted so that his ear was on a level with the opening. Voices inside, a man's and a woman's, but they were in another room somewhere and he could only make out a few of the words—not enough so that there was any sense to them. The man's voice was angry, though, that much he could tell. Angry and threatening.

McQuestion eased his head up and around for a quick look through the glass. The room was empty; he couldn't see the man or the woman or tell from which room the voices were coming. Until he identified the man, he still could not take the chance of going inside. He stayed where he was, listening, watching through the window. Waiting.

Better than five minutes passed. The man in there seemed to be working himself up into a rage; his voice grew louder, the words more distinguishable. He called the woman a bitch, and worse. She no longer seemed to be answering him. Then there was a sharp smacking sound; flesh striking flesh. The woman cried out, cried out a second time. Something crashed to the floor; something else shattered. The woman began to weep brokenly. The man bellowed more obscenities at her; he sounded half out of his head with fury. There was fury in McQuestion, too, of a different kind. He was coiled watch-spring tight inside, his lips skinned in against his teeth.

Then, abruptly, the man quit yelling. McQuestion heard the hard, angry pound of bootfalls coming his way. And a moment later, the man stomped through a doorway into view—big, red-haired, clean-shaven now. But even without the bushy red beard, there could be no mistake that he was looking at William Thaxter.

McQuestion pulled his head away from the window. His fingers were tight around the butt of his revolver. The bootfalls came across the room within; there was the sound of a door being wrenched open. Then he heard Thaxter on the front porch, heard him come down off of it.

Three strides brought McQuestion to the front corner, to where he could look past the porch railing. Thaxter was stalking away across the yard, toward the lean-to at the near end of the corral. He wasn't wearing an exposed side gun and his hands were empty. But that didn't have to mean he was unarmed.

McQuestion let him get another ten paces away from the house, so that Thaxter was out in the middle of the yard with nothing around him. Then he came out around the porch with his revolver up, thumbed it to cock, and said loudly, "William Thaxter!"

Thaxter whirled around, his hands coming up the way a prizefighter's will—but they didn't reach for anything. He blinked, staring. Disbelief slackened his jaw when he recognized McQuestion. His eyes bulged, turned wild.

"Stand where you are!" McQuestion warned him. "Hands up over your head!"

Thaxter whirled again and ran.

The movement was so sudden that McQuestion hesitated a second or two before he reacted. He shouted, "Stop, Thaxter! I'll shoot!" But Thaxter kept on running, heading on a line for the corral.

McQuestion steadied his pistol with his left hand and fired, aiming low for the legs. His first shot missed; his second bullet ripped through Thaxter's left calf and knocked him off his feet, sent him rolling the last couple of yards to the corral fence. But it didn't keep him down: McQuestion, running himself now, saw the man roll under the fence rail into the corral. The horses were plunging in there, frightened by the shots. Thaxter avoided them, came up and dragged himself under the lean-to.

McQuestion didn't fire again for fear of hitting the horses. For a couple of seconds he lost sight of Thaxter in the shadows; he was almost to the fence when the man reappeared.

And now Thaxter's hands were full of a double-barreled shotgun.

An instant before Thaxter cut loose with the first barrel, McQuestion threw himself sideways to the dusty ground. The load of buckshot blew away part of one of the fence rails, missed him, and peppered the yard harmlessly. Still on his belly, McQuestion got his revolver up and fired twice. Both reports were lost in the second boom of the shotgun, but one of McQuestion's bullets had struck Thaxter in the upper body and the impact jerked the shotgun's long barrel skyward; the pellets came hailing down forty yards away from where McQuestion lay.

Thaxter dropped to his knees, let go of the shotgun, and went over on his back. The horses were half mad with terror now, crying and snorting and pawing the ground; but they shied away from Thaxter and the shotgun. McQuestion got to his feet. His hands were shaking; his fingers felt as if the nerves had gone dead in them and he had trouble holstering his weapon. When he went ahead to the fence he had to lean against it for a few seconds to steady himself before he climbed through.

There was blood all over the front of Thaxter's shirt, but the wound was above the left nipple: he was still alive. And still conscious. He stared up at McQuestion with pain-dulled eyes that had lost none of their disbelief.

"You," he said thickly. "The Mountie. But I killed you, you bastard . . . I killed you . . ."

"You killed plenty of people, Thaxter, but not me. You won't kill anyone else."

"Why ain't you dead, damn you? Why ain't you . . ."

The rest of the words died in a spasm of coughing. Blood came out of Thaxter's mouth; he was starting to choke on it. McQuestion bent to roll him onto his side. When he did that Thaxter tried to curse him again, went into another paroxysm of coughing, and finally lost consciousness.

McQuestion dragged him out of the corral, onto a patch of dry grass. Only then did he notice the woman. She had come out of the house and was standing in front of it, near the porch steps. She had made no effort to approach, nor had she made any sound.

McQuestion went to where she stood. Hester Coolidge was about thirty, he judged, blond, fair, comely in a faded, tired way—or she would have been if her face weren't discolored by bruises and one eye weren't swollen shut.

She said in a flat, dull voice, "Did you kill him?"

"No. He's still alive."

"That is too bad. I was hoping you had."

"He's wanted for murder by the Canadian North West Mounted Police," McQuestion said. "He'll hang; I can promise you that."

She nodded.

"Why did he beat you, Mrs. Coolidge?"

"He thought I had money to give him. He thought this was a wealthy farm. He thought I would take up with him again, as I did when I was a foolish girl." She looked away, out over the barren alfalfa fields. "He didn't only beat me," she said. "He raped me last night. I wish you had killed him, mister. I surely wish you had."

McQuestion thought about Molly Malone. And about the Indian woman Kayishtik. But then he thought: No, it's better this way. Let the hangman have him. Justice—that is all that really matters.

CHAPTER 18

LATE THAT DAY, from the telegraph office in Petaluma, McQuestion sent a pair of wires—one to Colonel Steele in Dawson City, Y.T., the other to North West Mounted Police headquarters in Ottawa. Both said the same thing:

WILLIAM THAXTER MURDERER OF MOLLY
MALONE IN CUSTODY HERE STOP THAXTER
WOUNDED AND CANNOT TRAVEL YET STOP
FLOYD LOOMIS MURDERED BY THAXTER IN
SEATTLE ONE WEEK AGO STOP FULL DETAILS TO
FOLLOW BY MAIL ALSO BY WIRE IF DESIRED
STOP WIRE INSTRUCTIONS CARE OF POLICE
CHIEF CANFIELD THIS CITY

CORPORAL Z MCQUESTION

Canfield, a middle-aged, ultracautious man with drooping mustaches, went with him to send the wires. After McQuestion had brought Thaxter and Hester Coolidge into town in the Coolidges' farm wagon, it had taken him a while to explain matters to Canfield's satisfaction; the chief still wasn't quite ready to let him out of his sight. For all of that, however, Canfield was an efficient lawman once you got him primed. Thaxter's sexual assault on Hester Coolidge was more than grounds for Canfield to lock the man in a cell, which is what the chief had done. He had also summoned a doctor to tend to Thaxter's wound and seen to it that Mrs. Coolidge was treated and given a place to stay the night in town.

Thaxter had been conscious during most of the ride in from the farm, and most of the time since. But he hadn't volunteered a confession to the murders in the Yukon; all he had had to say were obscenities directed at McQuestion. But a confession wasn't vital; McQuestion knew all he needed to know about the deaths of Molly, her two helpers, and Floyd Loomis. As it was, his testimony alone would be sufficient to convict Thaxter of multiple murder.

When he and Canfield left the telegraph office, the chief finally seemed ready to bestow his trust. But he did suggest the Continental Hotel for McQuestion's lodging, and he did walk there with

McQuestion and wait to make sure he registered. And he did, just before departing, suggest that McQuestion not leave Petaluma without notifying him first.

McQuestion ate in the hotel dining room, even though he had no appetite, and then went upstairs and sat in his room without lighting the lamp. His job was done, but he felt no peace yet. There were matters still to be dealt with.

It was time to think about George Blanton, alias Evan Borcher.

Molly could rest easy in her grave now—but what about Eileen? Could he just ignore the fact that Blanton was alive and running free? Could he live with himself if he *didn't* go after Blanton again, settle accounts with him as he had settled accounts with Thaxter, put Eileen at rest too?

Perhaps it had been more than simple coincidence that had led him to meet the Longwell sisters; perhaps it had been an act of Providence. Perhaps part of his destiny was to bring George Blanton to justice.

And he could do it, too. Blanton wouldn't fool him a second time. Blanton would not get away again no matter how far he had to chase him.

The thoughts kept pounding away at him as he sat there in the darkness. *End Blanton's freedom, make Blanton pay, get Blanton, get Blanton, get Blanton . . .*

* * *

By morning he had made up his mind. He didn't need to wait until he received word from Ottawa or from Colonel Steele; he knew what lay ahead for him with the Mounted Police, had finally admitted to himself that his future there was in serious jeopardy. He couldn't go back to the Yukon now—not now. He had come to a crossroads in his life, and there was only one fork open to him, and he could take it because it was the way he had to go.

He returned to the telegraph office and sent a second wire to both Steele and Ottawa:

FURTHER TO WIRE OF YESTERDAY COMMA
EVENTS OF PURSUIT OF THAXTER AND LOOMIS
HAVE FORCED DIFFICULT DECISION STOP
EFFECTIVE THIS DATE I MUST REGRETFULLY
RESIGN FROM FORCE FOR PERSONAL REASONS
STOP WILL REMAIN HERE PENDING INSTRUCTIONS
ON THAXTER BUT REQUEST YOU SEND SOMEONE
TO HANDLE EXTRADITION STOP WILL ALSO
DISCHARGE ALL OBLIGATIONS INCLUDING
TESTIMONY AT THAXTERS TRIAL STOP THIS
DECISION FIRM I CANNOT RESCIND UNDER ANY
CIRCUMSTANCES

ZACHARY MCQUESTION

Outside, he walked along the estuary, where it was quiet and he could be alone. And for the first time since Molly's death, there was a kind of peace in him.

When he was free to leave Petaluma he would return to San Francisco and call on Della Longwell, as she had asked him to do—not a courting call, but to offer to accompany her back to Montana. He thought she would understand why he was going there if he chose to tell her. She might even be able to help him begin his hunt.

No one else was likely to catch up to Blanton in the meantime. If he hadn't left the northern states five years ago, he was not about to leave them now; he would still be there, somewhere in Montana or Idaho or the Dakotas, or not far across the border in Canada. Sooner or later, McQuestion would find him.

Thaxter first, and now George Blanton . . .

Bill Pronzini was born in Petaluma, California. His earliest Western fiction was the short story, *Sawtooth Justice*, published in *Zane Grey Western Magazine* (11/69). A number of short stories followed before he published his first Western novel, *The Gallows Land* (1983), which has the same beginning as the story, *Decision*, but with the rider, instead, returning to the Todd ranch. Although Pronzini has earned an enviable reputation as an author of detective stories, he has continued periodically to write Western novels, most notably perhaps *Starvation Camp* (1984) and *Firewind* (1989) as well as Western short stories. Over the years he has also edited a great number of Western fiction anthologies and single-author Western story collections. Most recently these have included *Under The Burning Sun: Western Stories* (1997) by H.A. DeRosso, *Renegade River: Western Stories* (1998) by Giff Cheshire, *Riders Of The Shadowlands: Western Stories* (1999) by H.A. DeRosso, and *Heading West: Western Stories* (1999) by Noel M. Loomis. In his own Western stories, Pronzini has tended toward narratives that avoid excessive violence and, instead, are character studies in which a person has to deal with personal flaws or learn to live with the consequences of previous actions. As an editor and anthologist, Pronzini has demonstrated both rare éclat and reliable good taste in selecting very fine stories by other authors, fiction notable for its human drama and memorable characters. He is married to author Marcia Muller, who has written Western stories as well as detective stories, and even occasionally collaborated with her husband on detective novels. They make their home in Petaluma, California.